SHORT STORIES OF TODAY

SHORT STORIES OF TODAY
BY TWELVE MODERN ICELANDIC AUTHORS

TRANSLATED BY ALAN BOUCHER

ICELAND REVIEW LIBRARY

PT
7487
·E5B6

Layout and cover by Gudjón Eggertsson, Auglýsingastofan hf.
Typesetting by Prentstofa G. Benediktsson
Printed in Iceland by Videy.
Published by ICELAND REVIEW
Reykjavík, Iceland
1972

Contents

Cruelty 9 — Halldór Stefánsson

The bottomless pit 14 — Gudmundur Daníelsson

The wet meadows
of Brokey 20 — Jón Dan

Weeping on an
autumn morning 26 — Ólafur Jóhann Sigurdsson

Nothing to tell 33 — Jakobína Sigurdardóttir

The infant,
the dog and I 44 — Jón Óskar

The market 52 — Geir Kristjánsson

Men at sea 57 — Jóhannes Helgi

The valley 66 — Indridi Thorsteinsson

Kitchen
to measure 75 — Svava Jakobsdóttir

The pass 81 — Hannes Pétursson

Night visit 88 — Jökull Jakobsson

Introductory note

The choice of stories in this small collection, for which I admit sole responsibility, has been limited by length. Within these limitations I have tried to make it as representative as possible, though much whose quality would otherwise have demanded inclusion has inevitably had to be omitted. The stories are arranged in order of the date of birth of each author, as in my earlier collection of modern Icelandic poems. I hope they will give some idea, in miniature, of what is going on in writing today in Iceland, where the pull between past and present is so crucial.

I thank the authors — whose indulgence I crave if I have done less than justice to their rich and sensitive language — and the editors of Iceland Review for the opportunity of presenting these works to English-speaking readers.

Alan Boucher
Reykjavík 1972.

Halldór Stefánsson

Cruelty

He cantered over the bumpy moor, hopping up on the humps of ling and down in the grass hollows — sometimes straight, and sometimes a little off-course — with a dog at his heels. He was full and happy and looked forward to coming home with a dog. The animal loped after him, tongue lolling, lethargic but eager to please. Sunshine all round, and half the Sunday to spend at will. Was it surprising if he cantered? Besides, he was not alone, he had a dog with him; an old thing, it was true — lazy and a little moulting — but a fine dog all the same. The boy stooped and gave it a sharp pat, as though a pleasant memory had been awakened in his mind. For a long while he had not felt so good as he had since making friends with this dog. And now he was taking it home on a brief visit — half the Sunday — in the sunshine. What fun, and really how immensely important, too. This journey was a kind of triumphal progress at the end of a long war, and now it was vital that it should be a success. The dog was not his own, but he didn't really mind if some happened to think it was.

There was not far to go: just across this moor and the dunes, then down to the beach on this side of the village. And there was sunshine and a Sunday colour over everything. Only the mountain on the other side of the firth was black, throwing a shadow far out on the water. But what does a traveller care about black mountains or faraway shadows when there is sunshine, it is Sunday, and he has a dog?

On reaching the dunes he changed speed, throwing back his head and sprinting hard. The light wind lifted his mop of yellow hair and his broad, ruddy face shone in the sun. As he ran he emitted an odd, nasal humming. The dog also mended its pace and looked up at its lord and master with brown, submissive eyes.

The sprint across the dunes was soon over, and they came down to the beach. Here there was a change in the runner's behaviour. His steps became hesitant and his expression uneasy, while the humming stopped. The dog quickly conformed to the pattern of its master.

The boy had caught sight of five children — three boys and two girls — a little further out on the beach. Some of them were sitting on rocks, the others standing. An embarrassed silence seemed to possess them all, as if some game had gone wrong or there had been a disagreement.

He was obliged to pass these children with his dog, but he had no desire to meet them. They were handsome, well-spoken children — almost too well-spoken. They were no playmates of his; they were his enemies. It might have been otherwise, had he been otherwise . . . had he been able to speak as well as they. But he was cursed with a cleft palate, and could only make himself understood with the greatest difficulty. Many misunderstood him deliberately, for it was amusing — for them. They put words in his mouth for him, and then everyone laughed — except him.

At first he had sought comfort from his mother, and she had advised him to stay away from those wretched kids. But he knew they were not wretched kids. They spoke so well. He was a wretched kid himself because he was different from other children. But why did he have to be? For this he received no explanation from his mother, except that it was God's will. After that he lost his respect for God and classed Him with those who were arbitrary and autocratic.

It was strange that when he read to himself, the words had the beautiful sound that he heard all about him. But when he tried to imitate that sound, he couldn't produce anything but this hollow hno-hno.

He could sing well, too. When he hummed the deep notes it was if a silver bowl had been inverted over a musical-box. But the children knew ways of humiliating him.

"Do you know the words?" they would ask innocently.

Yes, he knew them. He knew all songs and poems; loved all language; memorized words he heard or read. He took pleasure in forming beautiful sentences — in his mind. But when he sang the words, the questioners had achieved their purpose.

"Hno-hno," they laughed, and his singing was completely spoiled.

He looked at the girl who had admired his singing, hoping for support, but she had no wish to be coupled with him against the well-spoken. She tossed her head sulkily and laughed even louder than the rest, shrieking hno-hno.

After that he took his mother's advice and avoided the children. In any case he had nothing from their companionship but tears by day and waking fits by night.

But it seemed as if the children couldn't do without him. After a while they became bored with games in which all could speak equally well. Then they would come to him; invite him in a friendly way to join in, and he allowed himself to be persuaded. And in the heat and merriment of the game he would forget himself, and it wasn't long before a spiteful hno-hno was ringing all round him. The spell was broken, and he was all the more deeply wounded because he had been tricked.

This summer he had enjoyed perfect peace of soul. His mother had found him a job up in the country. There were no children there, only an old couple who said little and never laughed — and also this dog. It was the best companion the boy had ever had. He made long speeches to it in choice, beautiful language and read poems to it, and the dog never even smiled.

The boy now approached the children hesitantly. He meant to walk past them in silence with his dog and surprise them. No one was going to persuade him to join them or play with them. He had no intention of letting himself be tricked again. He was a man with a dog now — no longer had any business with kids.

His steps became brisker with these thoughts. But no sooner had the children caught sight of him than their idleness vanished.

"Hno-hno with a dog!" they cried, and they formed a circle about him.

"What's his name? Can he fetch a stick from the water?"

The boy broke through the circle without a word and whistled to the dog. But the others were not going to let such a quarry slip through their fingers. They coaxed the dog down to the water's edge with a slapping of thighs, calls of encouragement and whistles; a stick was spat on and hurled out into the sea, and the dog commanded to fetch.

The creature waded out a little way, excited by the boys' behaviour; but this was a country dog and did not know about fetching from the sea. It simply stood, up to its belly in water, and barked after the stick.

"Hno-hno," echoed one of the boys in a barking tone, and the dog's barking was almost drowned by laughter.

"He's got a cleft palate, too. Did you teach him to bark?"

The boys circled about him, baying hno-hno at him, while the girls shrieked and doubled up with giggles.

He stopped whistling and calling the dog; threw himself down on the shingle of the beach, and began to cry with loud, hollow sobs. Never had he been so cruelly treated; so badly betrayed. Dogs were treacherous brutes and never would he trust one again, however friendly its behaviour. They were spineless curs . . .

When there was no more victory to be had, the children melted away — not with noisy triumph, but indifferent and showing no signs of compunction.

The dog emerged from the sea, shook itself, and sat down sagely beside its master, as if ready once more to give a hearing to his speeches and poems, after that brief interlude.

A few drops of salt water splashed the boy's face.

"Go to hell, you cleft-palated brute," roared the boy in his handicapped speech. And he aimed a kick at the traitor.

The bottomless pit

This story is about the Fen, the bottomless pit, and the boy.

"Boy," said the milkmaid straightening herself with the pail, "undo the hurdle. I've finished."

The boy obeyed without answering, and while the ewes ran out through the opening he stood silently by the hurdle-post and waited until the pen was empty. Then he strolled off after the ewes. His job was to watch over them. He was ten years old.

Humming, he sauntered after the ewes and swung his piece of rope at the hummocks by the way. He was still on the stony ridges to the south of the farm where sedges grow in brown-green clumps and are the principal vege-tation, with the grey moss. And he continued on his way. No one thought of stopping here. This could be seen from the many parallel tracks. Every foot that treads the ridges is a passing foot, on the way to better land.

The Fen — who knew it as well as he did? No one — no one. For though you have maybe made your way across it, you will now remember nothing but its rusty red mud, spongy moss and lack of beauty. The boy remembers all this, too; but so much more besides. Summer after summer the Fen was his whole world, and to tell the truth, neither you nor I ever possessed a bigger world, though living in a city — maybe not even Einstein in America. So big is the Fen to those that know it.

He had now reached his destination. He stood on the high crest of the ridge and looked out over the marsh. It is not very extensive. It lies among a group of ridges, bordered by ridges on every side. There is not a farm to be seen; not a sign of human habitation anywhere — only the blunt brown ridges all round.

The boy stood still for a long time, allowing the ewes to scatter. The glorious day was just beginning.

There was a level tract overgrown with rushes close at hand. It was of a different colour, as if blue and green and black were combed together. He had sat there for a long time the day before, weaving the blades into webs. He had woven thirty-two webs, using about a thousand blades. The day before that he had stayed by the water and plaited sedges. But what would he do today? Make birds' nests? Gather snail-shells from his father's peat-cuttings? Watch the spider on the tussock beside the bog building its palace? No, these were all good ideas, but the best was still unmentioned.

He started off eastwards over the marsh, slowly, carefully, with head lowered. It made some difference where you put your feet, when they were bare and the Fen beneath them. There was many a hummock hiding painful spikes: birch-twigs here; rushes there; not to mention the pink-legged spider that is larger than the tigerbeetle and fiercer than a lion. The safest were the patches of yellow pond sedge, both shallow and soft and so pleasantly warm in the sunshine. He approached the middle of the marsh, wading through a whole mass of flags and skirting a patch of red mud. Suddenly he had come to his goal. He was standing at the brink of the bottomless pit.

The bottomless pit. Countless times the boy had stood here before, drawn by the hypnotic power of the place, his heart divided between a grip of dread and the power of a seductive suspicion. What was it, there before him? It was an eye. A single dark blue eye with yellow-fringed lids of moss stared up at him and tried to hypnotise him. And if one day it should succeed — what then? Then — then no boy would bring the ewes south over the ridges that evening, and down there in the darkness — there far down in the bowels of the Fen a small body would lie, ever motionless. Could that be what the bottomless pit wanted?

Silence.

And the dread increased its grip; would have torn him away, while the sweet suspicion held him fast. Something rushed past the boy's ear — something rustled in the sedge behind him. It was the breeze. A southerly breeze passed over the marsh, breaking the clouded pupil into a thousand fragments. But not for long. The stillness returned after a while to heal it.

Now it is clear, thought the boy, and moved a little closer. Seldom had this depth seemed clearer to him than just now. But what was that moving down there in the half-light? Oh, oh, beetles! The water beetles of folk legend. There came twelve of them, moving together in formation, heading upwards towards the sunshine. The boy clasped one hand to his mouth. The other gripped his rope. The creatures had now reached the surface. Were they intending to travel right up to the sky and attack the sun? No, ah no: they stopped short at the surface, stuck their sterns up out of the water, and dived down again. A tiny gleaming star seemed fastened to each shining black body and to vanish with it into the deep.

"They're fetching sunshine, so it won't be so dark for them down there below," the boy concluded, breathing more easily. "Or else someone sent them." But who? No, no one could answer that. Who knew what the Fen was hiding? And once more the breeze passed by, now from the north, and the eye of the Fen was broken and blinded anew. And so it went on, endlessly; change after change.

But unluckily there was no longer peace for a while;

the ewes had seen to that. They were now scattered far and wide and had to be herded together for fear of being lost. So the boy wandered off.

He finally drives them up to the edge of the marsh, and soon the heat makes them sleepy. They lie down, eyes half closed, and chew the cud. All is now well in the pasture and the boy feels he can relax a little. He climbs a short way up the grassy slope and finds a hollow carpeted with crane's bill and lady's mantle.

"Lulla — by . . . lulla — lulla — by . . ."

"Who's that humming?" asks the boy's soul; "who's humming?"

"Only me," answers the wind. "I'm humming a lullaby to the crane's bill and lady's mantle."

Now my ewes are asleep, and everything is asleep, except the eye of the Fen — the bottomless pit, thinks the boy; and maybe the wind replies: "I don't mind humming for you, too, fair-head. But the lady's mantle and crane's bill are my flowers."

The boy lies down among the flowers and turns his face towards the east, looking across the marsh. It is all green; pale green, blue-green and yellow-green. And there are the rushes with their colour, too, and the cotton-grass with its colour. And yet this Fen would not be a world apart, but for the eye — no, without that it would be no more than an ordinary, harmless marsh that never cried out to you, either waking or sleeping.

Silence.

Now the boy slept, hands under cheek. Slept and dreamed. What did he dream that day? Who can tell? Perhaps of the marsh sedge — that he was sitting by the water and plaiting sedges — or weaving rushes into webs. Perhaps. But there were other possibilities. Last year he had dreamed about a white mare with wings. She came flying from beyond the ridges and plunged into the bottomless pit. When he woke up he knew that it must have been an elf-mare, and he was not sorry for her, though she had been killed. But after that he had feared the pit even more. — No, there is no telling what the boy dreamed that day.

Days passed. The summer passed and the Fen was gradually touched with the grey pallor of autumn. With each day its complexion changed — everything changed with the coming of autumn, exept one thing: the bottomless pit! In staring interrogation, in deathly silence, it gazed up at the day, affecting it with its influence: a seductive suspicion; a vague dread.

Then one evening in September the boy stood at its brink for the last time that year and stared down into the darkness.

"Death", it entered his mind — "this is death looking at me. It lives down there in the marsh and keeps calling to me. But it shall not have me."

No, the death that dwelt in the marsh did not have that boy, for life held him by the hand and kept him from falling. He was only allowed to approach — to feel its presence and sense the mysterious shiver that it breathes into one's breast. Oh, what a relief to turn one's back on it! What a joy to flee from it!

For two more summers the boy watched his ewes in the green Fen, and each day was a new story, and yet ever the same: Life and death played for him, and life was glorious because death played too. But when the haymaking was finished — when he was twelve years old — there was to be a great change. One night his father's riding-horse went too near the bottomless pit in the dark, fell into it, and was found drowned the next morning.

"I should have filled up the bog last year, as I had intended," said the farmer. And he went with one of the men and they shovelled lumps of turf into the slough. "You won't take any more lives," he remarked when the work was completed.

But the boy — what did he say? He said nothing. No, not a word. But strangely enough he longed for the Fen no more. It had lost its power and its essence. Admittedly he went there a few more times, but he walked as a stranger, for it was no longer the same marsh. The bottomless pit had vanished; the deep, mysterious eye; the dread in one's heart and the seductive suspicion — death.

Yes, all that was gone now, and at the same time — at the same time the enchantment of life was gone. And the Fen-boy now looked for it elsewhere.

The wet meadows of Brokey

1.

"Look in at Bjóla."

Those were the words her mother spoke to her when she said goodbye at the edge of the village. She had thrown a scarf over her head early that morning and seen her on her way. With tears in her eyes she had admonished her and prayed God to keep her. She was the best mother in the world, but there was no need to worry just because her daughter was going away for the first time in her life to be with strangers. She would look in at Bjóla.

Like a traveller in the fairytales, she has food and new footwear, for there is a long way to go. It is early morning still and Akranes lies behind her, the dunes ahead. It is low tide and she walks dryfoot across the estuary. A long way before her lie the mountains of Hafnarfjall and the Heath Pass; beyond them, on the other side, is Andakill, where she has been engaged as summer helper. The farm is called Brokey and the master is old, but he has a young son. She has never met them, but has heard various things, and this will be the first time in her life she has been with strangers, though she is only the tiniest bit apprehensive about it.

About midday she met a man on the road and asked him if the farm on the edge of the marsh was Bjóla.

"That's it," said the man, "and aren't you little Magga from Outer Cottage?"

"Yes," replied the girl.

"Then you'll be looking for me, my pet," said the old man. "I'm your so-called father."

"How do you do." said the girl. "I'd never have known you; changed so. Did you get the message from Mamma?"

"Yes, I got the message from Mamma. And of course I'll keep you company, since we're both going to Andakill. No need to ask a favour. Oh no, of course I will. You'll be nineteen now, if I remember rightly?"

"Yes, I'm nineteen. It must be nearly eight years since we last saw each other."

"Yes, the old man hasn't been much for wandering; not a particularly dutiful parent. Eirik of Bjóla has a reputation for anything but that. And that mother of yours? Quite well, I dare say?"

"Yes, quite well," she said, laughing like her father.

"And the daughter means to take the Heath-Pass road, and no less, right up past the Trollwife itself. A bit scared, I dare say."

"No," she said smiling. " Not scared at all."

"You're not without pluck; no shrinking flower to look at, though you're no handsomer than your old Dad. But you'll not be used to much walking, I dare say?"

"Not used to much walking," she repeated.

"Haven't walked many mountain roads, eh, my pet? Not the Marsh road, I dare say? Nor the Keel road between the glaciers? To say nothing of further afield. I don't mention other roads. But in Berrydale, maybe, just for amusement?"

"That's right. But I've never been away from home before."

They walked on for a while and she glanced at him out of the corner of her eye. He tramped beside her, puffing in his beard. Soon he broke the silence.

"And so you're going to work at Brokey."

"Yes." she answered, "Mamma engaged me to work at Brokey."

"There's a young man at Brokey, pleasant-speaking, but a heart-breaker. Take good care of yourself at Brokey. I can believe you may sometime brook a brisk breeze there."

"What do you mean?" she asked, laughing. "I don't understand you. You are comical."

"Comical? It was a pun — a play on words. I like to play with words; wrestle with words."

"Your're so comical," she repeated, laughing.

"Comical? People have called me a rogue and a thief, a fox and a philanderer. You call me comical. Comical daughter."

She laughed loudly. But the man's expression became grave.

"Take care of yourself at Brokey," he said. "The son is crafty, but don't believe all he says. He never leaves a woman in peace."

"I don't want to be left in peace," she replied playfully.

"You're child, not a woman."

"This autumn I'll be a woman."

"Don't wish for it. And don't take on anything of your own free will. My pet. Never seen him, I dare say?"

"Seen whom?"

"The son at Brokey?"

"No."

She tried to look serious; then said, "there's one thing that worries me. Are there wet meadows at Brokey?"

"Yes, there are wet meadows at Brokey."

"That's bad," she said. "I dread working in wet meadows"
    Have we reached the Heath-Pass road yet?"

"Not long now; not long now," said the man. "This daughter of mine wouldn't be getting tired, I suppose?"

"No," she cried, jumping out of the road. — "Look at the wagtail. Now I'm going to ask it a question:

"Greeting, little wagtail mine,
Where is Swallow, your sister fine?
Across the ocean, spinning lawn?
That will Swallow your sister do.
I shall give you the berries blue,
If you tell me true
Where I shall be
Next spring and summer
And autumn and winter, too."

"It hasn't flown up," said the man.

"Then I'll throw my shoe at it," she said and sat down on a hummock.

2.

The weather is chilly when she sets off homewards in the autumn. For a long time she walks, alone and silent. She sits down to eat her lunch: she is in no hurry, for it is today that the old man her father is to come to meet her.

At last, opposite the Snout, he appears limping along outside the road in the scree.

"Hallo, Father," she said, "I'm glad you've come. I was beginning to get tired of trudging along alone here through the mountains."

"Hallo, little daughter," answered the man. "The young one wouldn't be scared, though, I dare say."

"No," she said.

"Mind you don't fall," said the man. "It's rough walking. And terribly steep besides."

"I'm watching my step," she replied.

They walked on for a while without speaking. Then the man broke the silence.

"Your hand is not as silky soft as it was this summer, I see. Hard work, I dare say?

"Yes," she answered, "the work was hard."

"There are wet meadows at Brokey."

„Yes," she said, sighing, "there are wet meadows at Brokey."

"Wasn't your old father right when he warned you against the son at Brokey?"

"Yes," she said, "you were right."

He stopped and looked at her. — "You have changed, sweet daughter; you're different from what you were this summer. Nothing has happened, I dare say? Nothing, eh?"

"No," she said, shrugging her shoulders, and continued, "— it's just that I'm a child no longer. Now I know myself; now I know him . . . and still I don't understand."

"Don't understand?" he said after a moment's silence. "It takes a good deal to understand. I was never exactly an innocent — no blessed angel; but not really bad, eh? Who does understand? You've no cause to grieve . . . no real cause, my daughter dear. That's the way it is with people, and life."

"Ah well," she said. "But I'm tired."

"You'll not be going to Brokey again? Not next summer? You'll find no fortune there, eh?"

"No," she replied, "I'll find no fortune there. This winter I'll be at home with Mamma."

"You should come to me next spring; some time early in the year. Come to the old man and help his old woman. We're so old. I'll slip you bit of pocket-money, my lamb."

"I'll be at home with Mamma this winter," she said.

"Next spring, early in the year?"

"I'll be at home with Mamma this winter," she repeated. "I'm not well and shall be at home with Mamma this winter."

He stared at her. Finally she looked up and said in a low voice:

"Next spring? I'm expecting a baby next spring."

"Just the same," mumbled the old man quickly and peered at his feet. "Just the same. You've no cause . . . no real cause."

They walk in silence, and the weather begins to change

as snow-clouds pile up over the mountains, and only the motion of walking keeps them from shivering Later they come to Bjóla and stop by the fence to take leave of each other.

"I don't know that I'll be seeing you often." she says. "I'd better ask now whether you'll be making your way to Andakill next summer."

He says nothing, but gazes at her with moist, reddened eyes.

"I haven't made up my mind," she continues, "but the farmer at Brokey asked me to come and work for him next summer. I haven't made up my mind, but if you happen to be going that way, then . . ."

But he is at a loss for words. He looks at the ground.

Then she says gently, "I'm so dreadfully tired. Could I come inside and sit down? I'm so dreadfully tired. It has been a hard summer. They're so wet, the meadows at Brokey."

Ólafur Jóhann Sigurdsson

Weeping on an autumn morning

Today I have been thinking about weeping. I heard it on
a still autumn morning with an overcast sky and a profound, melancholy peace that rested over the countryside
as everything faded and withered, taking leave and dying.
I remember still how certain I was that I would cherish
that autumn morning in my memory and retain its sadness
in my heart to my dying day, for I felt surrendered to a
kind of fading and withering myself as we waited for the
country bus and had nothing to give each other at parting.
I thought I would never know another happy day, nor ever
forget how we stood, looking in turn at the ground at our
feet, over the ling on the moor, and at the bushes on the
ridge beyond, where the colours of transience were like a
dull, dying fire, all but extinguished. I believed that my feelings beside the silent, provocative highway would never be
clouded by the mists of time; still less merged with the
past like a leaf with the soil, giving way to other feelings,
other experiences. I was so young and sensitive. Or, to be
more exact, so immature. Today, however, I am convinced
that I would long ago have forgotten that autumn morning, forgotten the parting with my friend by the highway,
had it not been for an old woman, huddled on the ground,
who started weeping.

We had walked in silence along winding tracks where the
night frost's blue transparency had not yet thawed in the

hoofmarks that were deepest and most distinct. He walked in front; I followed behind him. The weather was neither warm nor cold, but every now and then a cool fragrance could be detected in the air, especially when the track cut through areas of closely-growing bush or thicket, where faded leaves tumbled on to the moss and branches were left bare and dripping. Each time I drank in that cool, autumnal smell I dreaded the walk alone by these long, winding tracks, when I had taken leave of my friend and turned homewards. My friend was leaving home. He would not be turning back, for all the prophesies of disaster and protests of his family. He was to seek his fortune in a strange place and become a famous man, while I was seeing him on his way, going a little beyond the end of the homefield so that I could talk to him in private and wish him good luck on his journey. He was leaving empty-handed, but I was sure that he would become a famous man.

"You have come too far," he said in a still, colourless voice when we had followed the track for an hour and were only a short way from the road; "it's too bad to be dragging you all this way."

"Oh no," I answered in a voice like his; "it's not every day I'll come this way with you."

"Perhaps we'll be seeing one another soon down south," he said cautiously, and glanced over his shoulder as though to console me. "Who knows whether I won't be able to find something for you in the south."

"Now, in the slump?" I asked doubtfully, and tried to suppress the certainty that I would never be able to run away from my obligations if — as seemed very unlikely — he happened to find me a job in the south.

"There won't always be a slump," he said. "One must look on the bright side."

He had said the same many times before, always looking at me with a smile, as if to encourage and teach me to overcome all obstacles; but this time his words sounded strangely hollow in the clear stillness that seemed only waiting for a final wintery downpour to extinguish the last fire in the bushes. I could not repel the suspicion that he was no longer encouraging me, but addressing the clouds that lay over the land, or the red leaves that tumbled on to the moss; for he neither smiled at me now nor stepped out of the narrow path so that I could walk beside him and discuss the future. In reality he had already taken leave of me and of the dreams that had linked us since childhood and contained our world within a single horizon. He had broken all bonds, resolving to set out into uncertainty, with nothing to sustain him but his own belief in himself and his purpose: he was going to become a famous man.

Later we stood by the highway, chewing stalks of catstail that had lost all juice and flavour. We were waiting for the country bus, and both discovered that we had nothing to give each other on parting. It was as if the stillness about us grew heavy with this dismal knowledge and forbade us to utter a word. We just looked in turn at the ground at our feet, over the ling on the moor, and at the bushes on the ridge beyond, where the colours of trancience merged and melted into one another. I remember thinking something like: never shall I know another happy day, or forget how it felt when our horizon was cleft in twain before we parted.

At last he broke the silence, pointing to the north and saying, "Here comes the bus!"

I removed the withered catstail from my mouth and looked northwards too, until I caught sight of the light grey country bus in the far distance as it tore along the road with fateful speed, vanishing into a shallow declivity, only to reappear on the long, rounded ridge, racing through the fading thickets with cold, ruthless singleness of purpose, growing ever larger and more distinct as it drew nearer to us — two friends who no longer shared the same horizon; the same world.

"Well," I said awkwardly, "now **you** are going."

"Yes," he said, nodding. "I'll be in Reykjavík this evening."

"Are you looking forward to it?" I asked.

"Of course," he answered, his eyes still fixed on the bus. "Of course I'm looking forward to it."

"You're bound to find some sort of work in the south," I said. "The slump can't last for ever."

"No," he replied, "one must look on the bright side."

I pulled another catstail, chopped it apart with my teeth, and immediately spat the tasteless stalk from my mouth. The bus was now so near that we could hear the hum of the engine when it emerged from the dips between, where the leaves tumbled from the bushes and left the branches half bare and dripping. I felt myself surrendered to a kind of fading and withering.

"You ought to be coming too," my friend said in a voice that was unnaturally loud, and he picked up his bundle from a hummock of grass to be sure of not forgetting it. "You should have made a clean break."

"It's impossible," I answered dully. "I can't now."

"But when do you expect to come?" he asked, hitching the bundle under his arm.

"I don't know," I answered. "Perhaps you'll drop me a line soon?"

"Yes," he said readily and took up a position to signal to the bus, which was drowning the peace of the morning in a crescendo of roaring and rattling. "I'll write you a long letter, as soon as I've got myself fixed up."

"And you think you'll be able to find me a job?"

"Definitely," he replied.

I had intended to confide a small matter to him on parting, but found it difficult to put into words on the spur of the moment, and moreover had no time to turn it over in my mind. The country bus had scarcely drawn up when an old woman almost tumbled out of it and staggered to the side of the road as though she was blind. A younger woman with painted lips and shining slides in her hair followed her.

"You'd better sit down here on the grass, Mamma," she said.

"Oh, dear Lord," moaned the old woman, and was sick where she stood. "Dear Lord," she repeated between retches and groped in the air with her hands. "Hold my head, Sigridur, I'm falling."

She collapsed on the roadside after bringing up all she had eaten before starting that morning. I saw that she had had wheatcakes and been in too much of a hurry to chew them properly, for some of the lumps were as large as krona pieces. She took a white handkerchief from a pocket in her skirt and clenched it in a blue, trembling hand, but lacked the will to wipe her mouth.

"You'll get all muddy, Mamma," said her daughter. "Try and sit on the grass, off the road."

"I can't," said the old woman. "I feel so dizzy."

"Of course you can," said her daughter. "I'll support you."

But when she had sat down on the grass she began to retch again, and asked for a drink of water. I got a rusty can from the driver, ran to a nearby brook, filled the can and carried it to the old woman. She wiped the rim with her handkerchief, raised the can to her sunken, toothless mouth, and drank a few sips. There was a mouldy smell about her worn, threadbare country clothes, and the mud of the road had spotted her skirt and dirtied her sleeves below the elbows. "I should never have come, Sigridur," she moaned reproachfully. "They can't do anything for me in the south."

"Don't make such a fuss, Mamma," her daughter said, and she looked in turn at us and at the driver, as if asking us to take no notice. "You'll soon be better."

She re-arranged the slides in her hair, smiled awkwardly and sniffed. "Try and stand up, Mamma," she said, bending over her. "We mustn't make the driver wait any longer for us."

"They can't do anything for me in the south," whispered the old woman. I want to go home."

"Don't be so difficult, Mamma," her daughter said. "Can't you see that the people are waiting for us?"

"I want to go home," the old woman whispered repeatedly. And then she lay down on the ground, huddled together, and started weeping.

She wept quietly and weakly, trying to hide her face in her blue, trembling hands, and the pain in her movements expressed something of the defeat of a whole generation. I had never heard weeping like that before. It was as if the heavy clouds and ambiguous haze of all autumn mornings were condensed in it or had chosen it as a refrain to the transient colours and the soft, dying leaf that frees itself from the branch and tumbless silently on the moss. It was as if she were telling us her life story in that weeping; explaining that her travels were long past; that they had never really been travels at all; it was just a misunderstanding and mere folly: no one could do anything for her anywhere on earth; it was best for her to go home. We stood by her in silence for a long time and listened to her weeping, and when she had told us her life story to the end and had no tears left for the withered grass, we supported her to the bus and lifted her gently to her seat. Only after the bus had vanished into the distance did I realise that I had forgotten to wish my friend a good journey. I found it so strange that he should be travelling with that old woman.

Today I have been recalling all this, as so many times before. And it never occurs to me to reproach my friend, though he hasn't troubled to send me the letter for which I have been waiting many years, and which I have still not given up all hope of getting, some time in the future when he has become a famous man. But maybe the company in which he launched out into life had something to do with his laziness in writing; the company of a generation that was finished with all its travels, and knew they could do nothing for it in the south.

Nothing to tell

They sat face to face, across the kitchen table, over steaming cups of coffee, and the visitor seemed in no hurry to go.

It was true she had often been there before and drunk coffee in this same kitchen, but now it was as though she were seeing it for the first time. Surreptitiously, she inspected the freshly painted walls, spotless white curtains, little refrigerator in the corner, mixer on the working-top, scrupulously clean cooker. The four stools were neatly painted. Everything in this small kitchen was clean and well cared for. And the mistress of the house herself was part and parcel of it: a small, elderly woman, on the plump side, silver becoming predominant in the dark hair, complexion amazingly fresh, a warm, serene expression with just a trace of playful mockery in the eyes from time to time.

"Our good seamen have nothing to complain of now," she remarked. "Quite wonderful weather, day after day."

"Yes. God grant it bodes no ill," replied the visitor.

"Why should it bode ill?" asked the hostess smiling. "Are you one of those people who always expect the worst, and especially when all goes well?"

The visitor laughed. "Oh dear me, no. It's just that one is so used to every sort of weather here in the Flow that one finds it hard to believe that fine weather like this can last for long. But Sigrid, there's something I want to talk to you about . . ."

"Well, I dare say it's not so weighty a matter that you won't manage to get it out," said the other. "Do try one of these, my dear. I've nothing decent to offer you with your coffee, I'm afraid. I meant to make some doughnuts today, but got so behind that I had to leave it. So there's nothing but this rubbish from the baker."

"Well, of course I would have enjoyed your doughnuts, Sigrid dear, but this is really quite good. Yes, your doughnuts . . . you make such superb doughnuts, I've often meant to ask you for your recipe."

"Oh, I've no recipe." The hostess seemed eager to disclaim any credit.

"I don't believe it. I've often tried them, and they are always the same: quite the best I've tasted anywhere. And my Jón says so, too."

"I don't think he has ever tasted my doughnuts, Elin dear, so you must be exaggerating." Sigrid's eyes danced playfully. "At all events, I remember nothing about it."

The visitor protested vehemently. "Do you suppose I'd make things up about my Jón? He has often said that I should get your doughnut recipe. And the fact is that I'd have done so long ago if I'd not been a little bit jealous about his preferring your doughnuts."

They both laughed. "That's something to be jealous about," said Sigrid with amusement.

"I dare say you know the best way to a man's heart," said the other, who now had a responding twinkle in her eyes. In other respects she was unlike her hostess: a younger woman, slender and well groomed, with makeup and fashionably styled hair. Sigrid wore thin plaits in a bun at the back of her head.

"And was that what you wanted to talk to me about? My recipe. which is really no recipe at all? Because I'm telling you the truth, Elin. I've never weighed or measured for my doughnuts. I make them just as I always used to in the days when we had no scales and they were a special holiday treat — they and the old pancake fritters."

The visitor became serious again. "No, of course you didn't bake every day," she remarked significantly. "By the way, what was it called, the place where you used to live?"

"Saebol." The other answered in a lowered voice, as one might name a departed friend. She offered the visitor more coffee.

"Was it a big farm?"

"Big? Oh, I don't think it would called big by present-day standards. But it was a difficult place. And isolated. That was what made the difference."

"I see. You couldn't manage. And so I suppose it's deserted now. All that district where you lived before you came here?"

Sigrid replied quietly: "Yes. It's all deserted." And after a moment's pause — "The children didn't want to stay — and so there was no choice."

"No, and I suppose it couldn't have been much of a life." The visitor gazed almost greedily at this woman she had known for so long who had suddenly become a stranger; not just part of a cosy, well-kept kitchen, but something else as well.

"No, it wasn't much of a life," she said, speaking into her coffee cup. She saw it in her mind: a man alone in a boat, landing through breakers; chilblained hands; ragged children; meagre meals; an abundance of hot tears in a hard winter.

"No, not much of a life," she repeated and looked at her guest.

"As a matter of fact, it was about your home district that I wanted to talk to you," said the other meaningly.

A momentary shadow passed over the face of the older woman, the the eyes became playful again. "Really? You're going to write something about the poor wretches who gave up? But we were only family among eighteen."

Elin laughed. "I write! No, that's the last thing I'd dream

of doing. Oh no, it's for the evening coffee meeting of ours in the club. Inga Hreins had promised to talk about her journey to Switzerland and Italy the summer before last, but — would you believe it — she's off again next Wednesday! She and her husband, that is. Those folk don't stint themselves. And nobody knows where all the money comes from."

"Oh, I believe in people enjoying themselves. And I think they're nice people," said Sigrid, apologetic on behalf of this vagrant couple.

The other appeared slightly rebuffed. "Do you know them?"

"No, only by sight. But I like the look of them. There's something so friendly and pleasant about them. And so straightforward. I love to see them together. They're just what I think people should be: full of goodwill towards everyone."

The visitor looked relieved. "Well, I've noticed nothing special about them. And they say she doesn't mind being given an eye by others than her Lalli. But, as I said, she has let us down — and it occurred to us in our entertainment committee to turn to you instead."

Sigrid stared at her guest in astonishment. "To me? And what am I to do?"

"As you're from that kind of place, where all has been abandoned — yes, and one understands that it was all so special and — well, I don't know how to put it — so interesting that people should have been able to live there and — well, you're just like other people now that you're here, but — oh, I'm afraid I can't make you understand what I mean. It's just that one feels that folk who live in places like that can't be quite the same as others."

"Folk are much the same wherever they live, Elin dear, except maybe they're a little different in the way they dress and speak. The folk at home were neither better nor worse than other people, and life was a struggle for most, those years, both there and in other places. No, I'm afraid I've nothing to tell — no more than anyone else. The same hardships that everyone suffered."

— No more than anyone else, she thought, looking into her coffee-cup. Most of us have graves out there which are no longer tended. And most of us have a dead patch in our hearts where a thread was broken. There are no words for that.

"No, of course it wasn't much of a life anywhere in those days," the visitor admitted. "But all the same, it must have been a little special, in such an isolated place — and in the shadow of those mountains. I've sailed past that coast, and oh, those mountains looked terrifying to me!"

"Those were my mountains," said the hostess gently into her cup. Then she glanced out of the window and smiled: "But now I have these mountains, too. My folk are all her now — those that are still alive — and 'where your treasure is, there shall your heart be also'. No, Elin my dear, I've nothing to tell."

"Oh don't talk such nonsense," said the guest, jocular; "something must have happened up there that it would be fun to hear of. In places of that kind people have experiences that are utterly foreign to us — especially the younger ones. And then there are all those odd characters — both men and women — we so often hear about —"

"I'm sure they've written books about all the odd characters in Iceland by now — and if others haven't, they've done it themselves. So there's not much for me to add. At all events, everyone in our district who was a little odd in our eyes has been written about — and made odder still. But then people like that kind of thing. Though they were human beings, above all. And maybe we're every one of us a little odd in other folk's eyes."

The other raised herself a fraction in her chair. "Yes, and I believe people are bound to be a bit different in places like that. Well, I don't mean everyone. You're just like the rest of us. But take Lauga, whom I've somtimes met here, for instance . . . And the same applies to — what's his name now, the old fellow who lives down the road in Tungata? I met him here once, too. Wasn't he a former neighbour of yours?"

"You mean Marino?" Genuine amusement filled Sigrid's face. "Yes, you could say that. He's my brother."

Elin gave her a quick, embarrassed look, but seeing no sign of offence — only the twinkle in the eyes, so candid and free from malice — she recovered her composure. "Well, I'd never have believed it. You must be much younger. And you're not at all alike. He seemed to me so completely — so completely different from you and your husband."

"He's five years older than I am — but we were always considered very alike at home. And we shared the same hardships . . ."

"Yes, that's what I mean . You must have gone through a great deal that it would do us all good to hear about. — Really, I mean it. Such a hard life in that sort of place . . . Struggling to keep up a large family. It must have been . . . well . . . quite heroic. Wasn't the poverty appalling? Well, I mean not with you in particular, but with people in general?"

"There was somtimes little in the larder and a cold hearth," said the other after a moment's consideration. "People accepted that. The thought of being obliged to receive charity from the parish could sometimes do a great deal to soften the pangs of hunger when food was short" — and as though to herself — "for the grown-ups; not for the children. For them, nothing but food would do. We never starved, though. We always had a few animals. But one would try to dispose of as many as possible in the autumn; far more than could be spared. So sometimes there would be little towards the later part of the winter. It's hard to see children hungry and have nothing to put in their mouths — whether they're your own or other people's."

The guest leaned forward to see the face of her hostess better. "I see. So generally people found it hard to find food enough for themselves and theirs?"

"Oh no, it wasn't like that. Though it was often difficult in the later months of winter for a time, if the sea failed us. And the late summer could be bad for those with no livestock. But of course the boats went out whenever the weather was good."

"And then the winters must have been dreadfully cold."

"Sometimes," the other conceded, and yet with reluctance, seeing in her mind a white carpet of snow that covered everything and creaked underfoot, sparkling in the moonlight like the star-sprinkled ballroom floor of a fairytale. And an endless expanse of smooth ocean, twilight blue, embracing the long shadows of cliff and mountain. The lapping of calm-weather waves on the shore, so soothing to the ear. All white, blue, pure.

"Didn't people sometimes die of exposure?"

"Exposure?" repeated the other, as if she could not understand the word. Then she seemed to remember herself. "No, that didn't often happen — and never in my time. No, the sea was the great danger. And yet I suppose our losses were no greater there than elsewhere. And the cliffs, to those who collected eggs from them. But what could one tell about that? The sea was our highway and our larder; had always been so, though the land had its food-cupboards, too. No, it was no worse there than it is here; it demands its sacrifices everywhere and at all times, now and then — but it gives in return."

"There, I know you've plenty to tell," exclaimed the visitor triumphantly. "And you'll do this for me, won't you. I have to arrange this item. You must do it. People are impressed by that kind of talk; it's so patriotic and somehow so educational to have something of that sort, at least every now and then. You tell us about the poverty and how the people lived and what they did for amusement; what they thought about one thing and another, and then it wouldn't be a bad idea if you could put in some real heroic story as well, for they always happen in places like that. And of course something moving. People love everything sad and beautiful — not those stories of poverty of the sort that these communists are for ever inventing about lice and dirt and cruelty and all kinds of unpleasantness that never really existed. For after all, people can be good and clean, even if they are poor."

"Ah yes, perhaps it's the same with them as with others; they think exaggeration is more likely to have an effect. As for the lice, I don't know so much about it being invention. There were plenty of them about everywhere. Of course you've read these books — I read so little myself — but I understood that they were always making out that the poor people were so good in spite of the lice. It can be hard to keep things clean, though, when all the means are lacking, and the heart for it as well. And it's nonsense to try and make out that all who might have been better were bad people, any more then than now. And especially out in the country. No, poverty made some worse, no less than wealth; it froze men's hearts. And those who had something were the first to leave, so they couldn't have thought they had much to lose. We that had least struggled on longest, so we must have had more to lose. No, Elin, we have no right to judge; we can't see far enough. But for me to set myself up there in front of you all — it's out of the question. You might find some man to do it. They have so much to say — and can do it better than we can. Besides, they were the ones that bore the brunt of it, while we just watched and prayed — that's a woman's lot, and hard enough it can be at times, as it seems to us."

"Do you really mean to refuse me this favour?" asked the visitor, amazed and offended at the same time.

Her hostess gazed past her, out into the transparent spring twilight, that insinuated itself between the newly lit street lamps, seeking refuge from the brightness. It is not the conversation with her guest so much as the evening calm, warmly interwoven with the hum of traffic, that touches a hidden corner of her mind as with a magic wand, so that it opens up unexpectedly with sudden pain and everything passes, veiled in a transparent mist: the hopeful mornings of spring; the marvellous dreams of summer in a faraway place; the threat of autumn with the shortening days; the hard white reality of winter; Saebol — the living-room that evening when all the worldly possessions of the family had been loaded on the post-boat to be shipped down south. She stands there in the empty room, an aging woman, mother of nine children, and all that was is no more. And yet it is all there: the silent imprisoned grief of days of misfortune; the gladness of days of sunshine; the happy laughter of the children; their likes and dislikes, wild excitement and tears; her own hopes as she trod this floor for the first time as a young girl. Dreams of the future, both hers and of the young man who has now grown old, have already servered the thread that still holds her fast to the same spot on the living-room floor, dirty from the last upheaval. She hears him calling outside and pretends to be making sure that nothing has been left behind. But nothing has been left behind. Nothing but vague dreams about all the things they were once going to do. Then she feels the thread snap — and it is all over.

"Do you really mean that?" repeated the visitor.

"Yes, Elin. I couldn't do it for you, however much I would like to. I can't say anything about my home at a meeting of that sort — can't tell about it, and have nothing to tell, either. It would be better for you to ask my brother Marino. He has sometimes composed verses for his own amusement — and I don't think they're bad — some of them, at any rate. Sometimes he has been able to say in a verse what the rest of us wanted to say, but couldn't find words for.

The other jumped to her feet, excited: "What, is your brother a poet?" she exclaimed, the offence of the refusal already forgotten.

"Not a poet. Oh no, I don't think he has ever considered himself that. He doesn't compose anything serious; just occasional verses for us, when we're in trouble or somebody is married or has an important birthday — we can understand that kind of thing — and about our home country as it was and as we remember it. When we are dead no one will make verses about it any more; so this is just for our benefit, while we live. And perhaps you'd be interested —"

"Of course, that's why I always found him so strange," said the visitor with enthusiasm, not appearing to hear the last remark. "Poets are never like other people. Do you think he would do this for me?"

The other considered. "It's quite different, telling something in a poem," she said. "If you like, I'll ask him for you."

"No, please don't bother," said the visitor, buttoning her coat; "it's quite unnecessary. I'd be glad to talk to him myself. Just to think you should have a poet for a brother and have never mentioned it to me. You're a close one, I must say, and to be quite frank I find it rather unfriendly of you."

"Oh no, my dear Elin, it wasn't out of unfriendliness. It's so usual for men to compose verses, just as it is for some people to be unable to tell about things" — and after a moment's pause — "or to have nothing to tell."

The door opened and a girl looked into the kitchen. She was tall, slender and attractive; dark-haired, but with a fair complexion. She smiled at the two women, and when she smiled, she seemed to radiate light around her. "We're going out for a while, Mamma; the weather is so beautiful."

Her mother's face mirrored the smile. "Very well, my love; as you wish. But take care not to catch a chill if the evening turns cold."

The girl smiled again. "Don't worry, Mamma. Are you going, Ella? Like to come with us?"

The visitor glanced involuntarily through the doorway past the girl, at the young man waiting out in the passage. "Wouldn't I be in the way?" she enquired archly.

"Not unless you mean to follow us to the world's end,"

answered the girl laughing. "But if you're on your way home, we're going the same way; — and we're not shy, are we?" — She looked at her boy and he smiled agreement. They were both very young. And the dim passageway was brighter because of them. The visitor was not going home, but she was going in that direction.

And when they were gone, the mistress of the house stood by the living-room window, watching her youngest with her boy and wishing them every blessing, as so often before: that they might be given strength to overcome all obstacles, whatever might lie before them.

When they were out of sight she walked back and forth across the room rather uneasily. Not on their account: God was everywhere and would take good care of them, no less than of her and those who were gone. And they were, both of them, good and lovable young people. No, it was Saebol. And yet, if she had stood on the same spot again, she would have cut the thread a second time. For what was a past without a future? And what were parents without children? It was only what might have been — — — Really she was quite happy here — and besides, this was her home now — —

But then to think that at the last one must be united with an earth from which one's bones were not bred. — She gazed through the window, her face in shadow. Then suddenly it lightened. Down the pathway came an elderly man, walking slowly, but with the hint of a former spring in his step, in working-clothes; weary. Sigrun gave a sigh of relief.

— All this overtime, she remarked to herself. — He'll be in need of a rest, I dare say. I'd better put the coffee-pot on. What am I thinking of? — She hurried back into the kitchen. — As though it mattered where they lay on the last night, so long as they were together.

But it would have been best of all to lie there.

Jón Óskar

The infant the dog and I

When I was ten years old I said to my mother, "I want to go into the country. I want to ride horses and drive cows and mow and rake hay."

"Well," said my mother.

And so one fine day I set off from home, and my father had lent me his big sea-bag, while my mother had packed it with the clothes I was to take.

To cut a long story short, before long I was many miles away from my parents, and about the time when the birds begin to roost in the calm of the evening I was undressing in a strange house.

This was no ancient farmhouse.

It was a brand-new building of concrete.

Several days passed by.

There was also an infant there. And it had only been alive for a year and a few months. It was an exceptionally beautiful boy, loved by all, especially his mother. But what about this child? Why is he in the story? Well, you see, he is the crux of the story round which everything revolves, like the planets about the sun.

My mistress was a young woman, and beautiful.

When she spoke to me she said, "My dear Nonni." She always said My dear Nonni and never anything else.

My master was a young man and he was also married to my mistress.

Now there's nothing out of the ordinary about a young couple having a baby. It wasn't that, but rather the fact that I was to look after the baby.

The call of the sandpiper is loud, and such a strange love song fills one with the oddest feeling, though one may be only a child. And one watches it fluttering its wings high up in the air, and it becomes quite obvious to anyone watching it and hearing its tremulous piping that without this bird there could be no spring.

But all the same it was a cold spring — undoubtedly sea-ice off the north coast — so the little boy couldn't be outside. In other words. I had to look after him indoors. It was early spring and just a faint dusk descended on the land at evening. But I was indoors looking after the little boy, except when I went out from time to time to fetch fuel or the like. And if anyone supposes that I had myself sent out into the country in order to look after an infant, they are mistaken. On the other hand, he was a beautiful child. I would play with him in a big room whose windows faced south and west. I played with him by handing him objects of every kind and showing him how they could be played with. Then I sat down on a bed that was there in the room. And after that I said to him, "Now be a good boy."

But if there wasn't rain and slush outside; if a soft wind whispered among the fence-posts of the dry yard and the clouds were sailing swiftly across the heavens, then I stood up and walked to the window that faced south, or the one that faced west, and I looked out. Outside the window facing west there was a tiny hill with a stone in the centre of it. A certain whimbrel — an expert entertainer — had taken to frequenting this stone. I was his friend and he was therefore mine. At all events, God alone knows why he should have frequented this particular stone rather than any other on which to whistle his delightful airs, all of which had the original — almost unearthly — quality always belonging to great music. Why, unless for my entertainment? For he knew I was musical.

But have I turned my back on the little boy?

The little boy's music is different from the bird's. He opens his mouth and emits a yell that would compete with the most cacophonous jazz-band of any night club in any big city in its ear-splitting quality. In other words, the infant has shat himself. So I open the door and call to my mistress:

"He's done it in his trousers."

And while this is being put to rights I pretend I must leave the room, turn the handle of the outer door, and slip outside.

But unfortunately it doesn't take long to change the trousers of one infant, and after a few minutes I am back again in the window facing west, while the whimbrel opens and shuts his bill on the stone on the little hill, though the day is drawing to an end.

But there are other days, and other whimbrels than this particular whimbrel abroad, and other birds than whimbrels; birds of various colours, both big and small. A wagtail has its nest somewhere nearby. I haven't really time to look for nests. There's an infant in the house here. And I have explained how I look after the infant. Though I haven't explained how I put the infant to sleep.

Gently, softly, like the notes of an organ borne from a church, the evening comes to me. A touch of twilight over the green earth, and a nostalgic and marvellous tranquillity in the twitter of birds abroad in the calm.

This is when I put the infant to sleep.

From outside in the spring world, the glorious world of the birds, their song is borne in to me; in through the open window — the one that faces south, for the wind is in the north, or maybe there's no wind at all and the song reaches me all the more clearly where I sit. And I'm not sitting alone. I am sitting with an infant in my arms; a beautiful little boy whom I'm putting to sleep.

Why shouldn't I sing, although I am only ten years old? There's no valid argument against my singing, just like the birds outside in their glory. Therefore I sing. But I sing very softly, and sometimes I stop when I hear that the singing outside is better. The little boy leans his head on my breast and probably thinks I'm a grown man, though I'm not even wearing long trousers; only shorts that reach above the knee. But I hug him to me as if I were his mother, though I am not his mother.

"Do you hear?" I ask him.

And very softly he answers, "Yes."

And then I say, "Now the birds are going to bed. Let's go to sleep, too."

"Yes," says the little boy, and he presses against me. I suppose he likes me putting him to sleep. I like putting him to sleep, too. I sing to him, and he clasps his arms about my neck. And I sit like this until he closes his eyes and I feel him getting heavier in my arms, and then it's good to know myself strong enough to stand up with him, heavy and soft, and lay him in his cot.

But soon the spring was no longer too cold for little children, and you might suppose that matters improved. But this was not so. The little boy was wrapped in all kinds of clothes. He was put into a black coat, buttoned up to the neck, and a cap placed on his head, while I was told, "Dress yourself well now, my dear Nonni."

And I, who was ten years old, do you suppose I obeyed when my mistress said, "Dress yourself well now, my dear Nonni"? Oh no, that I didn't.

I wore no underpants; only shorts, black or grey, reaching above the knee. I wore no stockings; just short socks, and no vest, but only a thin linen shirt, while a cap was the kind of gear for which I had no use at all. My shirt was virtually sleeveless. That was how I would go out, and no one was going to get me to wrap myself up, for wasn't it spring?

And out we would go, the two of us; out into the spring.

And we felt the cool breeze play about us, for we were in Iceland.

Children are filled with a new, wild vitality when they discover that the world is outside as well as indoors. They can stay outside for hours on end without wanting to go inside, and when they come in they want to go out again.

I hold the child by the hand, the little boy in the black coat with a cap on his head and his nose protruding under the cap. I'm almost always obliged to hold him by the hand, because he's so small. I hold his right hand or his left, and he has gloves on both hands, but I don't wear gloves in the spring. I don't care if there is ice in the north.

I lead him back and forth in the yard, then out into the meadow and back to the yard again, and so on without end. But though I said I was not concerned about the ice that floated in an endless expanse off the north coast, this was incorrect. The icy wind chafes my bare legs and pierces my thin linen shirt. If this had been a lively companion — one you could have fought with — it wouldn't have been so cold; but this is a year-old infant that can only be led by the hand, and that's the sum of it.

One day I said to him, "Don't you want to go inside now?"

"No," he replied.

So that was all, for the time being. But the next day there was more.

"Don't you want to go in?" I asked.

"No," answered the little boy.

But I didn't give in, for I wanted to go inside into the warmth. I had trudged innumerable circles round the house but could still not see the point of these journeys without someone to fight with.

"You're so cold," I said to the infant, employing craft. "You want to go inside, because you're so cold."

"Yes," said the little boy.

In his innocence he believed it was true.

After that we went inside and I said to the people, "He was so cold, he wanted to come in."

But we weren't inside for long. I had scarcely got reasonably warm before he wanted to go out again. Besides, he had never been cold at all.

My mistress pointed at my bare legs and said, "How can you be bare like that, Nonni my dear?"

"Pooh," I said, "I'm not cold."

So there we were, outside the door, the two of us, and started walking round the house again.

But the next day I employed the same device to get inside when I wanted to, telling the people, "He was so cold, he wanted to come in."

But I've forgotten to mention that there were other farms than this in the district, and I was often sent on errands to the nearby farms: short journeys, though it was good to be sent, for then there was no infant at one's side, but perhaps a dog running behind or before one and sniffing at the hummocks, while the golden plover cried here and there in the marsh, and all the other birds. It was a very short distance to the nearest farm, but I was often sent there. There was a small girl there, about my own age. She said, "Shall we go up on the moor and look for nests?" But I didn't answer her. She was from the capital and could sing. She sang Goodnight sweetheart and so on. But I was not in love. She could sing as much as she liked. I was only ten.

Have I forgotten the infant?

Wait a moment.

It was a cold day and I was wishing they'd send me to the next farm, but what was the good of wishing? However, I'd been forced to put on my jacket, for the cold was intolerable, whatever the whimbrel might say. But no human power, nor even the elements themselves, should make me put on underpants, let alone a cap on my head.

"I say," I remarked to the little boy when I could no longer stand the monotonous tramping back and forth, "don't you want to go inside?"

"No," said the little boy.

I walked on for a while. Then I stopped and said to him. "You're so cold. You want to go in."

"No," said the little boy.

God help me, I could no longer fool the child.

"You want to go in," I repeated.

"No," said the little boy.

Did I give up?

No.

I led him behind the house where I was sure no one could see us through the window, squatted down in front of him, took hold of him by the shoulders and — as if all charity towards mankind had left me, as if I had never put this child to sleep, as if I had never told him how the birds went to bed, as if I were a ten-year-old boy of flesh and blood, born of woman, no more — I gripped his arms and squeezed rather than pinched, for the arms were so thin. But when I looked at his face and saw that he was on the point of crying, I squeezed all the harder and shook him, and glorious kind of feeling possessed me at this, and I shook him as though it were a matter of life and death to make him cry. Then the tears began to stream down his cheeks, and in his eyes — his blue eyes — there was no longer anything but terror. And when I saw this I took him in my arms and laid my cheek against his and hugged him fiercely to me, as if this wasn't real — and all the same it was real. But then I heard a sandpiper somewhere overhead, and though its cry is a sorrowful one indeed, it had the effect of making me realise that this was no dream and I had no choice but to go on.

I took out a handkerchief and carefully dried the tears from his cheeks, so that no one should see that anything had happened. Then I patted him on the cheek very affectionately and said, "It's so cold here outside. Shouldn't we go in?"

"Yes," said the little boy.

And I took his right hand, a little child's right hand —

though mine is small, too — and so I led him inside, I ten, and he a year old.

And when we were inside I said, "He was so cold, he wanted to come in."

But while my mistress was taking off his black coat and gloves, I seized the chance to slip out into the chilly spring. When leading him in I had noticed a dog walking across the marsh. I knew the dog, old, thickcoated, with a white stripe down his front — and God had surely sent him to me.

I ran to meet him and saw him wag his tail, for we were acquaintances. And when I reached him, I threw myself down on my bare knees in the marsh and clasped him in my arms. I held him desperately, as children hold their mothers about the neck when they are frightened. But I wasn't silent. I spoke to him. I said, "My dear Rover" — for I had given him that name; dogs have to have names even when they are strays. — "My dear Rover, I'm so wicked." But I wasn't one to cry, and so I buried my face in the thick, dirty coat of the dog and waited for the end of the world.

And that is the end of the story.

The market

In the middle of the city there has always been a market. The houses round it crowd together, so that no one knows how many there really are. They have a grey look, as though they have long since realised that the surest protection against the caprice of time is neutrality. Their occupants are ever changing, for houses last longer than people.

Real colours are only to be seen in the market: gay colours, sombre colours, fiery colours, and cold ones, too. The market offers everthing you can think of, but it takes time to search, unless you are content with the commonest articles, such as food to eat. And what a variety of food there is in the market: what sausages and what sides of bacon, white as milk and a hand's breadth thick! slabs of tallow as big as mill-wheels; gleaming fruit and plump cabbages in heavy heaps; fish, dead and alive; curious red crabs and scalloped shellfish that seem transparent and pure as water when they are opened — all in bursting wicker baskets that smell of the salt sea (and yet the sea is so far away that it dwells in the minds of men only as an inkling). Whole pig's carcases roasted on spits, and you can also buy live porkers and live lambs with curly wool that were the dearest playmates of children the day before and were called by their own names. Also all kinds of poultry can be obtained there: geese so fat that they drag their bellies on the ground, and prefer to lie still. Here you can get hot bread straight from the oven, and fried bread fresh from the pan.

In the market there is everything.

Here you can get sweetmeats for the children in incredible profusion: boiled sweets like pink cotton-wool, striped rock, and lollipops on sticks; every kind of chocolate; ice-cream and mineral drinks, and also liquorice. Here they sell many-coloured balloons, and monkeys-on-sticks that even the grown-ups buy and keep as talismans.

Here you can find every conceivable sort of household article and other things of wood or metal. Also jewellery, from worthless trinkets to the most precious stones.

In the market there is everything.

There is every kind of amusement, too. For a long time there has been a man who lifts an elephant, and another who has trained himself to wrestle with a bear. There are men who swallow fire and gaping wide slide razor-sharp swords slowly but surely down their throats and into their stomachs. Others swallow broken glass and nails — from time to time they always have to roll up their shirts and show their bellies, for people have to see the scars of operations before they will take it seriously.

You can reflect yourself in mirrors that extend or compress you; weigh yourself and have your fortune told at the same time. You can try your strength and win a prize, and you can do so many things. You can climb to the heavens in a balloon or ride on the Great Wheel.

You can see men tie themselves in knots and walk on their hands with their heads between their legs. And then there are those that have themselves sawn in half, conjure rabbits out of thin air, and change water into wine.

Wine, yes; wine is to be had here, too, in great vats that stand on trestles and sweat in the sun.

In one place there is a kind of salient of the market between the houses, where they converge. Here, at the point of the salient, is an opening into the street of the women, which curves away secretly into the city.

The street of the women is so called because only women live here. And it is much narrower and more winding than other streets. For this reason it is not possible to see at any distance who is coming. And if two respectable citizens happen to meet accidentally in the street itself, it never goes any further. No wife or fiancée ever dares go out into this street after her man.

In the salient of the market-place the girls stand in rows dressed like dancing-girls. One can walk past and examine them without causing any scandal, and one can also exchange a look unseen by others. Even drunks are hardly ever seen entering this street openly, let alone men who are sober. They always make their way there by side streets, after examining the girls in the salient and exchanging a look with one of them. Then they sometimes stay for quite a while, and sneak away furtively in the morning with empty purses and memories of a hollow breaking of wind between bare chest and naked female breast.

In the market, too, revival meetings are held to purge men of their sins; even the great original sin. People come here to comfort themselves with God because they cannot abide men, and then there are others who have not fully enderstood their own needs, and therefore do not know exactly what they are looking for.

The market is generally crowded. People here are at the beck and call of their own desires, but do not think very much about that, or feel their dependence too keenly — except when they fail to get what they want. Here there are those who want to save and have such trouble in making up their minds, and here, too, there are those who buy and buy and buy, so much more than they need. Here there are lean old maids in long lace dresses buttoned up to the neck — they buy a little; maybe a handkerchief — stare, and are shocked by the sin and depravity. One is often aware of them in the crowd before seeing them; there is usually a faint odour of cat's piss about them, mingled with the smell that comes from clothes kept too long in closed cupboards. Here, too, is the man who is so gay and kind to everybody because he is so delighted with himself — always buying something cheap and gaudy and acting the clown. Here is the black-clad. big-bosomed and wordly-wise one, haggling for fish. When she gets angry, which she always does, her eyes are hooded and her features turn to a shield of hard, impenetrable metal. Only the mouth moves, workling like a mill, so her face ceases to be a face and becomes like some other impersonal part of the body situated above the neck.

Here there are young women who handle everything with slender fingers, flauntingly. They are accompanied by their husbands, who meet the world's gaze with young, proud eyes and seldom look at anything. Many of the women are pregnant. And here, too, are the aged breakers of hearts, with their bowlers and a white carnation in their buttonholes, who believe they are still young because the carnation is.

The cold-hearted one sits here, drinking, and he embraces and kisses with the most feeling expressions. This display of emotion always surprises people a great deal, though it is as assured and unfailing as the very sunrise. And the innocents cry in wonder, "How kind you have suddenly become!"

Men often come to the market straight from work with crumpled caps, never looking about them, but walking straight to one place, where they buy some ludicrous trifle, and are gone. There are also some who resort to the market to hide, and they start if anyone should slap them on the shoulder. Young poets walk there with eyes like wet bilberries, and there are men who beg for alms with mutilated limbs.

The market offers everything.

In the evening when darkness falls there is a firework display, so that the skies are filled with falling stars. Then there is dancing to music until morning on a glamorous platform where gaiety is supreme. It plays on some like a rosy spotlight, making them rich and beautiful; on others it is like cheap tinsel, while others look as though they had stolen it somewhere.

Then everything dies down of its own accord, and the voices fade . . .

But they have never quite finished sweeping when a new market-day begins, with crowds of new people who have not been there before.

Men at sea

The drifter Bryndís lies at the little village jetty ready to put out to sea, and by the end of the jetty, a brand-new sea-bag beside him, a boy in his sixteenth year stands gazing proudly up at a small red house on the headland. — No, of course not! His mother is not in the window. There's little danger that Kristrún on the Headland will make a parade of her feelings. Still, it wasn't much to expect that she might have stood there and waved goodbye. After all, this was his first voyage. His mother's face, cold and hard, flashes for an instant in his mind's eye. No, there's no point in standing here. He heaves the bag briskly on his shoulder and vaults to the deck.

"Stand by to heave to!"
They have reached the fishing bank, and the brown net — several tons of small mesh, lead weights. corks and floats — streams in the wake of the boat, until a line of green floats extends as far as the eye can see, with the red end-float only visible from time to time on the crest of a distant wave, while more distant still, out on the horizon, lie the other five dísar from the village, sister ships of the Bryndís.
Darkness falls, and nothing remains but to clear the deck for the night's drift. The engine is stopped, the door of the

wheelhouse closed, the hatches battened and the masthead light kindled.

The cabin is so small that there is no room in it for a table, so they have to eat with their plates on their knees; but it is cosy down there. The little stove crackles in a friendly way and its glow plays on men's faces, while strange shadows are cast on bulkheads and ceiling. Jökul, the skipper, sits without speaking. He is a taciturn, swarthy giant of a man with rugged features and is dressed from head to foot in black. The cook, a thin, delicate-looking individual, is also silent, but the engineer, who rejoices in the extraordinary name of Líkafrón, holds forth on national affairs. His eyes are grey and warm and his voice the most beautiful one the boy has ever heard, endowed with a magic that fills the cabin with a marvellous peace. The little crew allow the engineer to talk, nodding heads from time to time in agreement, but making no contribution. Finally Jökul speaks.

"Well, Már. Now it's time for you to turn in. You've the dog watch."

The boy crawls into his bunk and lies for quite a while listening to the waves lapping against the hull and the creak of cables above deck. The old boat rocks him gently and he is already beginning to enjoy himself. His last impression before falling asleep is of the rough voice of the skipper:

"I don't like this calm."

"Change watches!"

A light touch on the boy's shoulder and a hand on his wrist. He is wide awake in an instant. The skipper is bending over him, buckling a large wrist-watch on him. Jökul speaks in a low voice, as men do involuntarily among sleepers. "Wake us at four, and have hot water ready on the stove. And if we come close to another vessel, give me a call."

The boy makes up the stove, then goes on deck and sits

down on the edge of a hatch. It is a star-bright night: dead calm and dead silent, but for the creak of ship's timbers and the ceaseless lapping of water against the hull. It is as if the sea is whispering secrets — fearful secrets this night; for the old boat groans deeply and there is the trace of a child's sobs in the theme of the waves. In the eastern sky a wonderfully brilliant star is shining. The boy cannot remember having noticed it before. Out of the blue-black ocean, where he can make out the red riding-light of another vessel, comes the melody of the sailors' song from Capri: "Bella, bella Maria — men at sea a-fishing . . ."

Kristrún on the Headland stands barefoot in white nightshift at the little window, gazing absorbed at the mirrorlike expanse of ocean. At this time of night she is usually in bed, but tonight she cannot sleep. The day was a turning-point in her life; today she had put the final touches to the education of her son, and Jökul, the trusty skipper, would see to the next stage.

"Fifteen years," she whispers.

It was a long time, and yet so short when you looked back. Fifteen years since she came to this village, an eligible young woman of good family from a large farm in another district. She had eloped with the skipper Magnús, defying parents and relatives; a dark-eyed girl, enigmatic and secretive, who would have nothing to do with the village people.

The likes of it won't lead to any good, the old folk had said when they heard her story — and so it had turned out; not because the old folk are always right, but because things are like that — either getting better or worse. Within a year the young woman was a widow, and began working as an ordinary hand in the fish-yard. From the first her beauty had been a cause of considerable speculation among the men of the village, and of concern among the women in the same degree. Nor did her haughty manner improve matters, for now, when people would have shown friendliness, they met

59

only her dark eyes. She came down from the Headland at dawn and returned at dusk to her little boy.

Later came the depression and the misery that it brought in its wake. The villagers went hungry and the parish had to make occasional distributions of free food, but the woman on the Headland struggled on without assistance. In the course of a few years she aged, but the boy thrived, and what saved them from complete starvation were the bundles of fish that someone would lay at their door in the early mornings from time to time all through those hard years. Kristrún did not know who it was and asked no questions, but she suspected Skipper Jökul. So the years went by and the woman on the Headland gradually acquired a kind of legendary name. It was even whispered that she was a witch and the village woman used her to frighten naughty children.

Kristrún opens the window and lets the sea breeze play about her. Yes, the boy is in good hands. He will be with Jökul for two or three years and then go to the school of navigation down south. She dreams great dreams for her son, and with good reason. He is hard-working but gentle-natured, has done well at school and won most of the village prizes for swimming and other sports. No, there's no cause for complaint; the boy hasn't disappointed her. A warm wave passes through her body, as earlier that day while she watched him from behind the curtain when he stood at the end of the jetty, proud and handsome like his father, with that enchanting nobility about his head and shoulders. Kristrún saw him as captain on the bridge of a large ocean-going ship — her son!

She closes the window and goes back to bed, a faint smile on her lips — for the first time in many years.

The boy glances at the watch. Time to be moving. He stands up and now notices that the eastern sky has changed colour and gigantic, pitch-black clouds are banked up right across it. He hears a rush and looks up. A flock of white sea-birds passes over the boat at full speed heading towards land, while far off in space a star falls in a great arc. The crests of the waves no longer pat the boat like little children's hands; the outside of the hull is fiercely pounded and a pungent smell of brine is borne to him. A gust of wind snatches at his coat. The vessel lists and the lantern strikes against the mast. The boy looks about him before going below. There is no sign of land to be seen.

The skipper sits up in his bunk and listens. Each burst that hits the boat is more savage than the one before. — It's blowing up a gale! He swings himself out of his bunk and shakes cook and engineer. — "We must haul in at once."

"Shark!"
Jökul hauls in the net, many feet of it ripped to shreds, and soon they catch glimpses of this blackguard of the seas: the foam about the boat is full of them. The lantern beats against the mast and breaks, raining fragments of glass over Líkafrón.

The boat begins to pitch heavily. The stern lifts sharply, higher — higher; hovers a moment, poised high above the surge — then, dropping silently, as if through a vacuum, hits the surface with a mighty crash — and the sea rises like a wall of viscous green glass. The whole vessel shivers like a sick animal and spray rains downs on the men without intermission. The boy feels a sharp pain in his chest. His knees give and he falls on all fours, spewing into a broth of jellyfish and brine; a cold sweat breaks out over his body, but his arms and hands, peeling with jellyfish burns, quickly feel for the net again. This is his baptism of fire — he must prove himself. He shall, he shall! He heeds neither pandemonium nor shark's fin; is conscious of nothing but net and still more net. It piles up before his eyes, and with incredible persistence he continues to drag it behind the wheelhouse.

Suddenly the winch stops. The boy looks up. It is blowing gale force with blinding rain and mountainous seas. Three flashes of lightning in rapid succession illuminate the boat, and in the light he sees Jökul running with raised axe towards the counter, where the tangled net is dragging the stern under. There is a loud report and the tangle disappears. At the same moment the boy is aware of a fearful monster looming over the boat to starboard — a mass of water. Without ceremony he flings himself into the wheelhouse. He hears the cook yell, the sound of smashing woodwork, and the mizzen goes overboard.

"The boy!" He hears Jökul's wild cry. "Did he go over, too?" In the same instant they burst into the wheelhouse, the skipper and Líkafrón. Jökul seizes the boy in his arms. Waiting for a lull in the shelter of the wheelhouse, he runs with him forward to the cabin and orders Líkafrón to take him below, secure the door and douse the stove.

The engineer attacks the stove and has just finished putting it out when another wave hurls itself on the boat and the sound of breaking, up on deck, reaches them below.

Shortly after this the cabin door is beaten from the outside and broken in before they have time to open it. Jökul stands there, bloody in the storm, holding a lifebelt. He shouts something, but his words are swallowed by the wind. At the same time the sea breaks over the boat yet again, snatching the skipper away. The vessel lies on its side and the sea pours down into the cabin.

When the boy recovers his senses he finds himself halfway up the foremast, his legs entangled in ropes and wire. He clutches desperately to the groaning mast. The boat looks as if it has been raked by gunfire: nothing on deck left standing, except wheelhouse and foremast, in a welter of raging foam and rain. It is swept like flotsam from the trough of one wave to the next and the water level in the hold rises rapidly. The body of a man floats from the cabin, face downwards. It is the engineer.

"Líkafrón," cries the boy, "Líkafrón —"

The engineer makes no sound. He was drowned below. The body is washed across the deck, striking from side to side, and then, thrown up on the gunnel, it seesaws for a moment — and vanishes into the deep.

The water in the hold has reached the frame of the hatch and the boy sees that the vessel is sinking under him. He closes his eyes and thrusts himself even harder against the mast; harder and harder, until he and the mast are a single entity. — The firmament explodes in a clap of thunder, splitting the air above the boat with a violent crack. Bright lightning illuminates the sinking wreck, and, a short distance ahead, a foaming line of white breakers, and a rocky coast.

Up to noon of the next day the sister ships of the Bryndís come limping into harbour, all battered more or less. By evening Bryndís has not returned, and people are beginning to give up any hope that she may still be above water. Many dísar have been lost at sea. Every man, woman and child is filled with foreboding. The storm continues to rage, and there is no prospect of a search until it dies down.

In the house up on the Headland Kristrún sits, pale as a corpse, almost the colour of chalk, and stares at the convulsions of the sea. Rain lashes the house and from time to time spray is dashed on the panes as a heavy wave breaks on the rocks below the Headland. Her face is mask-like; its expression frozen; barely human. She sits in the dark all night long and does not move until a new day has dawned. Then she scans the horizon in every direction. The storm has died down, but not a ship is to be seen. Not a mast. Nothing, anywhere.

For a while the woman sits, paralyzed, in her chair. Then she pulls herself together sharply; stands up, trembling, and grips the window-frame so that her knuckles whiten. — That's how it is! — She trembles violently and presses a hand against her heart. — That's how it is! The boat has gone down, but her son alone has survived. He is young and tough. The others drown — her Már swims. He is young and and tough. — And Kristrún sees him battling in the foam. Lightning flashes, playing on his fair head, like platinum. — Her son can swim like a seal. — She weeps with pride and urges him on. — Onwards, Már! Onwards! — She continues to encourage him until the breakers wash him up on the glistening black rocks of a strange shore. She sees him stagger to his feet. The gale tears at his tattered clothes. He is half naked. — And with pride Kristrún sees the hardened muscles and brown young flesh — her flesh. He is handsome; the most handsome and the strongest of all the boys in the village, and he is coming back to her. — Kristrún laughs and cries in turn. — Now he is safe. There's a house near the shore. The people help him inside. They are good folk, but he is so exhausted that he falls asleep before he can tell them who he is. He sleeps the clock round — a day and a night, yes, that's only natural. And now he should be waking up, at this very moment, and telling them. And there would be a call to the telephone exchange. And the telephone exchange would send a message to her. — She looks at the clock. Ten minutes past eight. The telephone exchange has been open for ten minutes. — Soon the messenger will come running. — Már, her son, is coming back to her.

Kristrún totters out to the kitchen window — and a profound sigh is released from her breast. A boy comes running round the corner of the store, heading towards her house. She rushes into the hall and opens the outside door. Her bloodless lips move, but no words come. Then the boy hurries past the house, and Kristrún recognises him: it's the son of Árni the cooper, on his way down to the beach with a toy boat under his arm.

Kristrún staggers back into the kitchen. Her lips are still trembling, but gradually her features stiffen and once more her face is carved in stone — expressionless. She knows now that her boy will never come back. A pail is still standing in the middle of the floor where she left it yesterday morning. Slowly and stiffy she kneels beside the brush and pail. There is a sound of rasping against the rough wooden floor, with long pauses between — and the bristles of the brush are flattened under the heavy strokes.

The valley

1.

Dalsmynni lies under the pale slope on the eastern side of the valley, which penetrates the mountains from the south.

All is peaceful. There are rain clouds in the mountains, and the air is charged as before heavy rain.

The new house stands on a rise where the old smithy was. A little higher a cluster of ancient turf ruins crouches, humble and silent in its decay. In that old farm there was laughter and tears for a thousand years. It was the birth-place of a great family, now dispersed throughout the region and all over the country; a family descended from fourteen kings on the male side. Those ruins are now the haunt of field-mice, while the projecting bases of the collapsed walls are wetted elegantly by dogs nosing after bitches, and tufts of dead grass protrude everywhere between the fallen fragments, for no scythe ever comes near such desolation.

Looking farther up the valley, all the way until it narrows and climbs to the fells, the observer sees occasional patches of green. His enquiry will elicit the information that these are the traces of old, abandoned farmsteads. He may be tempted to wonder whether war has passed this way, killing men and ravaging their land. The answer would be brief and simple, though concealing a great tragedy: no wars were waged here, and no men wiped out; just a handful of folk destroyed piecemeal by cold and poverty; but so quietly and uncomplainingly that no one noticed.

There was a light knock on the door in this peaceful and almost deserted dale, sometime between the world wars. It was a young man who bade good evening. She returned his greeting softly and he asked for the farmer. The girl replied that he was not at home.

"But please come in," she added, drawing aside to let the visitor pass.

He went into the house before her, and when inside greeted the people there with a handshake. Not that there were many of them: just two more women; one of advanced age, the other in her fifties. The old woman sat on a bed, mumbling with toothless gums and rocking her body back and forth. The bedstead looked strangely antiquated in this new house.

Dissatisfied with the young man's silent greeting, the old woman voiced the unspoken question of all: "What is the visitor's name?"

He told them, and the girl's eyes darkened when she heard it. The middle-aged woman paused a moment in her work and gazing sharply at the visitor said, "Not the poet, by any chance?"

He hesitated, reluctant to acknowledge the title before the old woman. "I don't know what I should be called," he said. "People are sometimes given the name of poet without deserving it." He looked up at the ceiling, as if a blackened hook for an oil lamp might give him moral support.

"Oh yes, that's sometimes so. But you're not too bad, poor fellow; not such a fearful liar," remarked the old woman.

"Grandma!" exclaimed the girl, "how can you say that to a visitor, Grandma . . ." Then she fell silent, for the grandmother had begun to rock and mumble toothlessly again.

"Please take no notice of her," pleaded the girl. "She is old and . . ."

The visitor lowered his eyes from the lamp-hook and meeting hers said with a smile, "Why not take notice of her? She has had ten times more experience of life than I, and it would be strange if she weren't wiser."

"She has lived all her life up here in the dale," explained the girl.

The visitor gazed steadily into the girl's eyes, and he suddenly saw them brim-full of enchantment, like the summer night in the dale, when the reddened sky turns to molten gold that flows over the shallows of the murmuring glacial river below the farm. He said, "Yes, and for that very reason: for this dale is the centre of the world, and there is nothing outside that isn't in it."

"No, not such a fearful liar," muttered the grandmother, rocking back and forth, and she pursed her sunken lips in satisfaction.

The middle-aged woman now returned and leaning her head against the door-jamb stared at a point just behind the visitor. She was rather plump, but neat, and her eyes were brown and candid. She stared for moment and then spoke quietly, though her words filled the room and somehow seemed to linger in the air:

"Will the gentleman stay the night?"

He thanked her, touched by the friendly invitation. It was evident that the grandmother wanted to say something. She had stopped mumbling her toothless gums between rocks, and kept giving him side glances. All three of them were now silent; the only sound, the wind in the eaves outside.

"I hear they're fighting, down south there in Cholera," said the grandmother at last.

"Korea," the guest corrected.

"Oh I dare say it's the same. I've never been one for those foreign names. Besides, we're all so well educated these days that the skies won't fall though a backward old daleswoman can't say a word in any but her own tongue."

"You mean the world could manage to get along without you?" asked the girl smiling.

"I dare say," answered the grandmother, and the guest thought how old and tired her voice sounded.

"Yes," he said, ignoring the interruption, "the world is fighting over its prey."

"They should be ashamed of themselves," she said, shaking her head. Then she stood up slowly and on aged feet tottered out of the room.

After the guest and the girl had sat in silence for a while the middle-aged woman came back.

"You can go to bed whenever you wish," she said, and pointed to the door beside the living-room.

2

The sheets were cool and the seasoned woodwork of the bed creaked when he stirred. It was the kind of warm, dry creak heard when people move in bed, alone or with another. After a long interval of watchful silence he was aware of the lightest of touches on the door. Was it his fancy? No, he heard it again. Then a whisper:

"Are you awake?"

"Yes," he replied. "Come in."

She came in, closed the door behind her, and sat down on a chair by the bed. He turned to face her, and the creak of the bed brought agreeable associations.

She was pretty; a sturdily-built girl with broad hips, delicate features and a frank expression. She had prominent eyebrows and all her movements were graceful. And she exuded a warmth and tranquillity, offering trust to any who sought it, and from her body a delightful fragrance, due to no artificial perfume, that was the scent of her own flesh.

"Don't you think me forward?" she asked with pleading eyes.

No, he didn't.

"I wanted so badly to talk with you — you who come from out there, where the crowds are. Isn't that a wonderful life?" — And her face shone with eagerness for that wonderful life.

His eyes darkened, pupils reflecting the clear daylight of the summer night outside, and the girl in her pale blue nightdress. Then, speaking slowly and with emphasis, he said, "All that you call "out there" is misty and strange to you, but it shouldn't be called "life", it's too raw and restricted for that; too lacking in substance and tied to the passing moment."

"But it's so lonely here," she said.

He considered this briefly and then said, "Loneliness is painful; very painful. But the cure for that pain isn't to be found in being one head of a many-headed mass. Loneliness is the companion of those whose hearts are eaten with longing —"

He had been gazing out of the window, but now he turned to the girl and said "— and you want a boy."

"Don't say that. Please don't," pleaded the girl.

"It's true," he said shortly; 'and your boy will come. But don't let him take you away; you belong to this valley."

He gazed at the girl and she could see by his eyes that he had discovered something new about her. Straightening herself on the chair, she said, "Why do you look at me like that?"

The guest blinked and moistened his lips. "You are true," he said. "I've come a long way, and you have not disappointed me."

"There may be truer women than I," answered the girl, not wanting to seem conceited.

"That doesn't matter," he said. "In my eyes you are true — or rather, you are my image of truth, for this valley is in your eyes and this blue sky on your brow and the bright night in your blood. And your boy will come and you will make him belong to this valley."

"How beautifully you talk," she said staring at him in wonder.

"Because you came to me beautifully," he replied simply.

"Are all artists like you?" she asked.

"I'm no artist," he said. "I enjoy things, that's all."

'What are artists, then?" she asked.

"Men eyed with suspicion as oddities, and mocked if they won't stay tethered to the same post in their estimation of the merits of the great. And their art — that innocent delight and honest vision which they hold intact through the dust and heat of the day — is something that's not appreciated until it has lain for ages in dark mouldy museums as an ancient relic."

"Then why this enthusiasm of living people for such dead art?" she asked, staring open-mouthed at the guest.

"Art doesn't depend on that sort of enthusiasm, except on the surface. Its essence comes from within, demanding creation, whether that creation is acknowledged today or tomorrow."

"Then is there nothing but disappointment? Nothing bright or joyful? Is everything penned and haltered in the prison of old, accepted ideas?" cried the girl, surprised at her own eloquence.

"I'm afraid so," he replied; "but here in this valley you are saved. Here there's no need for anything to cast a shadow on innocent joy. The moist scent of the new-born calf; the richness of well-matured meadows after a shower; the coursing blood of the stallion — all these are innocent joys and you have them."

"I want to go, all the same. I want to see people and talk with people — many people," she cried.

"There it is again, that longing for something you haven't got; that longing like the thirst of dry soil for rain. You want a boy."

"Will you be my boy?" He saw how she blushed and lowered her head.

"I am sorry," he said. "Strong hands are needed in this

valley. Not mine. Mine are not the hands of a doer, but of a thinker."

The girl raised her head and looked out into the luminous night. It cast a reddish sheen on her hair, and her breast heaved, as though she were making a great resolve. She seemed to be staring at something very far away, beyond the blue haze at the head of the dale where night had been halted on its northward advance. And in his mind the guest began to compose a poem of the valley: a poem about the lovely girl who sits alone on a rock under the pale mountain slope and sings of her friend who is to come, and of her longing for him, and of the garland of flowers with which she will crown him. And she sings, too, of the shapely ewes wandering in the bright pastures, and the lambs gambolling about them. And she sings of the stallion that charges among the herd in biting, foaming passion; rearing and plunging in his mad game with the mares.

And to the guest this was the most exquisite of poems, and the song of the fair maiden sweet and consoling, with a cadence of the thousandfold harmonies of the dale.

3

He woke early, and the sun was shining on the dew-covered homefield, sparkling in a million particles.

He got up and dressed, and went outside into the brilliance of the morning, where all was veiled in a mysterious enchantment that promised a hot day. The air vibrated with a sweet chorus of song that came in waves along the valley slopes. And through this sound he heard a rhythmic beat, rapidly growing louder and its tempo rising as it approached. This was no fancy, he knew; no illusion in the morning calm. And as he looked north he saw a man, mounted and leading a second horse across the barrens. The muscles of the horses strained under the gleaming skin, glancing in the light, and the man leaned forward in the saddle, riding fast.

He had dismounted before they came to a halt; a brisk, swarthy man who strode up to the guest with outstretched hand, saying, "Good day to you, and who does us the honour . . .?"

The guest introduced himself.

"Ah, just so," said the man. "Such visitors are rare." And he walked back to the horses to unsaddle them.

The guest now remembered that he must be on his way and said, "Could you mount me down the valley?"

"Must you go at once?" asked the man. "It's not yet even time to be out of bed."

"Yes, I had better," answered the guest.

"Come in and drink coffee with me first," said the man. "The horses can do with a bite of grass."

They went inside.

The middle-aged woman was already up and about and had lit the fire. She stared when she saw the guest, but only said "Good morning" and hurried with the coffee.

"How do you like our dale?" asked the man.

"Very much."

"Yes, this is a good dale. Though some say that farming such valleys costs no less than staying in a luxury hotel."

"That's unjust," said the guest and there was despondancy in his voice. Then after a moment's silence, he added, "Here you have everything; more than can be had in any hotel. Not a staff of servants, it's true, but that could be called the self-indulgence of the deprived."

We have the blessed creatures." said the man speaking slowly, "and our bodies we can provide for ourselves. And no one needs to worry about vomit on the floor; we leave that out of doors if we ever find ourselves obliged to bring up our drink."

The guest smiled.

"Won't you stay on a few days?" said the man. "I promise you shan't go hungry."

It was a fair promise to the poet in him, but nevertheless he replied, "No, I'm afraid I can't. I came because

I wanted to see a desolate vally. However, I've come to the conclusion that it will be hard to find a valley so completely desolate that the desolation of those who don't live in valleys isn't greater."

And when they had drunk their coffee the guest took his leave of the middle-aged woman, bidding her say good-bye for him to the grandmother and the fair-haired girl. After that they rode away together, guest and farmer, and out on the barrens looking back he thought he could see a white hand waving; though only for an instant. And he thought again of his poem; the poem about the lovely girl who sat alone on a rock under the mountain slope and sang of her friend who was to come.

At the mouth of the valley poet and farmer took leave of one another. And the descendant of fourteen kings stretched out his arm towards the dale that lay behind them, green and warm in the morning sun, and said, "Since you are a poet, carry the greetings of our valley to the nation, and tell it that from these turf mounds a new people will rise, and white flocks will graze the slopes again, and in that new settlement none shall suffer cold or hunger; neither snow nor flood shall destroy men's property, for all those things are a nightmare of the past."

And after the farmer had said this, they shook hands. And their handshake was a warm one. And the poet was followed by his godspeed, and by the scent of the valley, deep into the crowded places.

Kitchen to measure

His name was Ingolf.

He was endowed with an imagination and creative urge beyond most men. All his spare time was devoted to invention. In this way he cultivated his unique talent and made sure that it did not rust in the dull monotony of everyday toil. He was never happier than when giving birth to an idea. It seemed to start somewhere deep down inside him and force a way up to his head. His body would become stiff, his eyes fixed and staring. The idea was taking charge. With this came an excited trembling, — a mounting impatience, as when a note vibrates on the highest strings before the fall of the conductor's baton. If the idea was one that could be put into execution immediately, the excitement became intense. From that instant the idea was supreme, and in the power of its boundless energy he became a superman.

His own preference was for building. Here there were innumerable opportunities for new inventions. And these were propitious times. Such times had not been known in Iceland since the Age of Settlement; everyone needed housing. And this common need of his fellow countrymen for housing established a bond between them. The nation was a united building team. Some drew up plans, others drove in nails; some were masons, while others wrote books or exhibited paintings so they could earn the money to build.

In this way other creative arts either directly or indirectly contributed to the art of building in the land. Never had the creative impulse of the nation enjoyed so comprehensive an outlet.

Three times had Ingolf built an apartment for himself and his wife. He began with a basement flat, and each time moved a little higher. He made money through these enterprises, because the country was in the grip of inflation; he was therefore now able to take the final step towards what had always been his objective: the building of his own detached house. He realised that now he stood at the parting of the ways. Now, for the first time, he could show what he was really capable of. His ideas had scarcely had sufficient scope in collaboration with others; severe limitations had been imposed on their execution. But now a door opened on new, unlimited possibilities. The ideas came thick and fast; ever thicker and faster. They swept over him like breakers. He was helpless driftwood at their mercy, sometimes dragged under and sometimes riding on the crest of the wave. But when he was finally washed ashore, he knew precisely what kind of house it was to be.

He quickly saw the vital importance of the kitchen, for the work performed there was the foundation of the whole life of the house. The kitchen was in fact the heart of the house, and if the heart stops beating death must follow.

It was not without a certain apprehensiveness that he approached the work. But he set to with single-minded determination.

He began by measuring his wife.

He measured her height in shoes, in slippers, and on stockinged feet. He measured the length of her forearm and upper arm, and of her hand, both clenched and open; to the figures obtained he added her height on tiptoe. In this manner he discovered exactly how far she was able to reach. He took her bust measurement and hip measurement. He measured her from the waist downwards, and, and he measured the distance between all her joints. He measured instep and length of stride. After that he sat for several days and watched her working; made accurate observations of her normal movements; how often she bent and stretched. He measured the speed with which she performed various tasks and how many paces she took across the kitchen floor. After that he sat up late into the night and worked on his measurements.

It emerged that his wife took many unnecessary steps in her kitchen work, and that many of her tasks could be more efficiently performed. The largest proportion of excess time went in bending down. The figures demonstrated this conclusively. It was quite clear: all bending down in the kitchen must be eliminated. But this was a problem he could solve; he sketched and calculated furiously. And finally the work was complete: from his measurements and observations the perfect kitchen emerged on paper.

About this time he happened to read in his newspaper of a German salesman of kitchen fittings who was on a visit to Iceland. This man was quoted as expressing his great satisfaction at business dealings with the Icelanders — they were exceptionally appreciative of the importance of kitchens. Many of their ideas in this field were so ingenious that his firm was seriously considering introducing them on the international market.

On the international market! This opened wider vistas than Ingolf had ever dared to envisage. It was as though a new power were poured into his limbs; the joy of creation fused with a childlike excitement, and in the wake of these came a strange sensation that made him uneasy at first because he was unable to identify it. It reminded him somehow of rain and fluttering flags. He knitted his brows . . . had he not felt something similar before, in his boyhood? . . . Yes, that was it: standing on a rock at Thingvellir on 17th June 1944, when the Icelandic Republic was proclaimed. He straightened himself on his chair. It must be patriotism. By his efforts the fame of Iceland would be spread throughout the world! He immediately picked up the telephone, and the German said that he would be honoured to be of assistance.

Later the same day they were facing each other across a desk in the office of the German's Icelandic agent. Ingolf explained his designs. He began with the potato bin. It was to be pivoted. Under the edge of the workingtop there would be a button connected to the bin. When this was pressed the bin would be opened and raised. In this way the housewife was spared having to bend down.

"Mein Gott," said the German.

"There's to be a similar device for the revolving dry-goods cupboard," Ingolf told him.

This was to be a circular unit divided into compartments. In the compartments there would be closed containers for the dry-goods. The unit would revolve inside the working-top and each container open as required. On the wall above there would be an illuminated control panel with buttons. When one button was pressed the flour-container would appear; another would produce the sugar, and another the oatmeal. Here also the housewife would be spared the bother of bending or wasting time fumbling in cupboards for the right article.

"Mein Gott," groaned the German.

And the mixer was to be built into the wall. The whisks would emerge from the wall like a crane. It would save space.

"Mein Gott."

The mixing-bowl would be mounted on a conveyor belt and could be brought to the housewife wherever she was standing in the kitchen. This would save walking.

"Mein Gott," said the German.

They went over the drawings, point by point. Ingolf forgot time and place and the German missed his dinner. By midnight, however, the kitchen had been fairly fully dealt with and the conversation moved on to doors. Strictly these did not concern the German, but uniformity of wood-work was an essential feature, as Ingolf pointed out. The

German asked whether it would not be best to do away with all raised thresholds.

"Raised thresholds?"

"Yes, I thought . . ."

"What did you think?"

"I thought . . . I thought your wife was a cripple."

Ingolf stared at the German And when the full implication of the man's words dawned on him, it was as if a precipice opened under his feet. He was falling. At the last moment he managed to drag himself back from the brink; realised how utterly mistaken he had been in his estimate of this German. There was obviously no need to waste more words; in fact he let the silence speak for him as he gathered his papers together and walked out.

He found an Icelandic carpenter to undertake the work. Needless to say, the workmanship was in no way inferior, but deep inside he was disappointed. His patriotism had been genuine and sincere.

He watched over the work like a mother over a sick child. He tolerated no mistakes. And when at last the kitchen of the new house was completed, he stood for a while in the middle of the floor with eyes shut. His powers had been wound so long to their highest pitch, and now that he could finally relax, he felt an agreeable torpor creep over him. It was finished.

For the first few days he all but drove his wife out of the kitchen. He experienced such unspeakable pleasure in being there himself, while at the same time it was as though he was glued to the kitchen floor by some profound spiritual intertia; he was filled with a vague misgiving: that nothing but emptiness awaited outside. Once he stepped over the threshold, what would be left? Could he ever create again? Was there anything more to create? He was afraid, and therefore he hung about in the kitchen. But he kept his eyes open, and time after time he caught his wife bending down to open the potato-bin by hand.

"The button," he reminded her; "press the button."

Then she would straighten herself and press the button, begging his pardon and saying that it was just thoughtlessness on her part; force of habit. It would come. But it did not come. And one day he lost his temper He roared at his wife, "The button. woman! Can you never learn?"

At this his wife sat down and burst into tears. The tears poured down her cheeks, over stainless steel, formica and control panel. They ran in streams down the shining hardwood. He had never seen such a disgusting exhibition. And as he stood in helpless rage, watching his wife cry, something suddenly began to happen inside him; something that forced its way up to his head. His body stiffened. His eyes became fixed. A total, overwhelming sense of elation possessed him. An idea was being brought to birth.

He must get a new wife for his kitchen.

The pass

They were giant, cold mountains and had occupied a broad promontory jutting out into the ocean. They were very old; had gathered there before the coming of the birds. Never had smoke from the hearthstones of man risen into the air of their valleys.

These ancient fells had long stopped talking together — they knew one another too well — and spent their days in watching and listening. They found the travels of man especially diverting, and followed his movements under the sheer slopes, watching and listening to his thoughts with tolerant amusement. In later times it was a change, too, to hear the rifle shots that shattered the silence in spring when the foxes' dens were besieged.

And this bright day of late summer a man was travelling through the fells.

They saw that he was scarcely more than a dwarf, for his feet did not reach the stirrups, which dangled back and forth when the horse broke into a trot. The fells burst out laughing — a gust of wind whining against the edge of the cliff. The man looked all about him uneasily.

However, the fells knew nothing of this man, nor was there any reason why they should: it was Gamaliel the saddler from Sandbakki, the village in the east, on his way home from town, and he had not passed that way before. He was wearing a black bowler-hat on his head, an old raincoat unbuttoned over his dark Sunday suit, and patent shoes that he never put on except when going south to buy leather. He carried his belongings in a small bag at the back of the saddle.

Gamaliel had set out with a boat that was to have put in at Sandbakki, but the route was changed, and he had been obliged to go ashore at the settlement of Grund. Luckily he had an old and faithful client in the neighbourhood: Jón of Brekkubær, who lent him a horse, saying that he would fetch it himself at the autumn round-up, for he had business over in the east. Gamaliel might leave his sheets of leather at Grund to be sent on by the next boat.

And so Gamaliel the saddler came to be travelling here alone in the fells And although he had sewed more saddles than any man in his time, he was unused to being on horseback; for he never left his village, except when obliged to go south and buy material — and this, moreover, he sometimes ordered by post. Not that he had any ties to hinder his leaving home; neither wife nor children to care for. Nevertheless he had the workshop, long his own, with the little room off it where he slept and heated himself a bite of food or made coffee. And in the workshop or his room was where he liked best to be. Although he was well thought of in the village he did not make a habit of visiting, except during occasional bouts of tippling that occurred on an average twice a year. Then he would lock the workshop and put a sign on the door: "Closed until further notice." But these interludes seldom lasted more than a fortnight, for by that time he was beginning to long for his workbench again and for the evenings spent reading in his room. When he lay on his bed with stories, old and new, of adventures and perils by land and sea he would realise how lucky he was in spite of everything: he owned mortgage-free premises and money in the Savings Bank; was the only saddler in the county and so always had plenty to do; could afford a dram fram time to time, when he would drop into other people's homes and drink a cup of coffee in the kitchen with the mistress of the house while the menfolk were away at sea or out at work — maybe even fondle her a little. On the other hand he was never happy in large gatherings — outdoor meetings, for instance, where there were crowds. He would rather stay at home and read. Though he enjoyed going to church on Sundays. Then he would sit up in the gallery, where he could lean over the rail and look down into the chancel, with a good view of the county sheriff and the doctor and their wives, and of the pastor's wife. Added to this, he was so close to the organ and church choir that he felt as if he were taking part in the service — though he did not sing — for the hymns broke over him in choral diapason like green billows, — lifting him high in the air it seemed, so that he forgot in spite of himself how low he was — and this could last for as much as five minutes. For this reason he looked forward to Sundays.

Gamaliel the saddler was now halfway home. He was beginning to feel tired, being unused to travelling. It would have eased his legs had he been able to thrust his feet against the stirrups, but this advantage was denied him; instead the irons dangled back and forth when the horse trotted, making him bad-tempered. It delayed him, too, for he dared not ride fast, being so unsteady in the saddle. He had almost fallen off when he tried to ride out of the yard at Brekkubær, in the grand manner, at a gallop. He had heard the children laughing and made up his mind to go carefully for so long as he could be seen. But when he was out of sight of the farm he decided not to give the horse the whip again, for safety's sake. — And now he was halfway. All things considered he could be thankful he was not riding a horse of more spirit.

When Gamaliel the saddler reached the narrow pass that wound upwards through the range — this was about an hour later — he felt a sense of oppression, for suddenly not a farm, or a living creature apart from a few sheep, was to be seen. The silence was absolute. Involuntarily he

gripped the pommel of the saddle with both hands, peered
ahead, and saw that there was still far to go. But the horse
jogged on and soon this feeling passed — for the most part.
He reassured himself with the thought that there was only
about two or three hours' ride left, after which he would
be at home in his workshop once more; the weather was
fine and still, the time just after one. Besides, perhaps he
had already crossed the county boundary; it must be somewhere thereabouts. But when he raised his eyes to the
slopes on either side of the gorge, the distance seemed to
grow longer, and before realising what he was doing he had
struck the horse a blow. It started sharply forward, the
stirrups swinging wildly against its flanks, while he clung
desperately to the pommel, convinced that every stream
he rode over must be the boundary.

Thus Gamaliel the saddler proceeded on his way; sometime slowing down to a walk, when he looked about him
and heard the wind whipping the ridges of the high fells
in gusts; sometimes at a trot, when he kept his eyes fixed
firmly ahead, as if hoping to shorten the road thereby. But
weariness was now beginning to creep up his legs and he
was hungry. Thorgunn at Brekkubær had provided him
liberally for the journey, putting a bottle of milk and a
large packet of sandwiches in his saddle-bag. But something seemed to whisper in his ear that it would be un-
wise to dismount. He might lose the horse. What would
become of him if he had to chase after it, far away up here
in the fells? And might it not be difficult for him to mount
again if he shortened the stirrups as he proposed to do?
Might it not take a long time to find a hummock high
enough? He felt in his pockets to assure himself that the
knife he intended to use for boring holes in the stirrup-
leathers was there. When he found it, he forced himself to
a decision, for he could not go without food altogether.
He pulled the horse to a halt in a green, dry hollow, dismounted cautiously, led the animal to a small stream that
ran nearby and let it drink; then back to a grassy bank on

which he sat down, pushing his hat on the back of his head, wiped the sweat from his brow, and glanced once again at the scree-littered mountainsides, an expression of hopeless apprehension on his face. He did not let go of the reins, though the horse began to nibble.

Gamaliel the saddler contemplated the steep slopes. The bank on which he was sitting was so high that his legs hung in mid-air, short and stumpy and shaped like the staves of a barrel. He felt farther away from his workshop than ever before, though he must have passed the county boundary — wondered that the landscape had not changed now that he was in his own county — and sensed in every fibre of his being that he was far from human habitation. If he shouted, no one would hear him. At the most the sheep would look up and stare, and then go on munching.

The horse nibbled at the bank. Gamaliel still dared not let go of the reins; clutched them like a lifebelt in the open sea. Finally he took the knife from his pocket, stood up, went over to the saddle, picked up one of the stirrup-leathers and was about to bore a hole in it. But as he put the point to the leather, the smell came to him as though he was in his workshop at home, and checked him: Who had given him leave to bore a hole in this leather? Wasn't this the saddle of Jónas of Brekkubær? Gamaliel stood stock-still for an instant. His hands fell to his sides. He stared into the distance and a weary look crept into his face, regret blended with a trace of bitterness clouding his eyes. Minutes passed, and then he unstrapped the bag from the saddle, took hold of the reins again and pulled the horse to the bank. Here he sat down on the grass, leaning his back against the bank, put one arm through the reins so that he could use both hands to open the bag without letting go, and began eating.

He wondered now that it should ever entered his mind to bore new holes in the leathers higher up than usual. Would that not have been a positive admission that he was quite incapable of coping with normal conditions? And wouldn't the Brekkubær folk have laughed when they saw what he had done?

As he drank the milk and ate the sandwiches he began to feel better. The slopes of the mountains no longer seemed to loom so near, or the road home to be so long. The horse stopped nibbing, for Gamaliel would not let it move. It hung its head and closed its eyes in the heat.

After Gamaliel had refreshed himself with food and drink, he got to his feet and strapped the bag back on the saddle. He was in the habit of lying down after every meal and so he succumbed to the temptation to sit down again against the bank and stretch out his legs. The autumnal sun flamed in the gap between the fells and the vegetation on the lower slopes began to redden. He saw that all the hollows about him were carpeted with berries, but though he felt the urge, decided not to pick a handful; he might forget himself, and the horse take to its heels.

Gamaliel closed his eyes and savoured his rest to the full, still holding the reins with both hands. He felt the weariness draining out of his whole body. The air was pure and when he inhaled deeply the sweet scent of the berryling was mingled with a faint, agreeable smell of the horse. And Gamaliel the saddler dozed off. But not for long. And when he started up, the horse was still standing in the same place, twitching an ear.

Just to be sure, Gamaliel looked about him. Then he shrank back suddenly against the bank, his face pale and heart beating violently. Right beside him, towering over him from a tall hummock, a full-grown sheep stood watching him. Its nose had been stripped of flesh up to the eyes and the bare bone of the skull was exposed. It stared at him.

Gamaliel went weak all over. The fells crowded in on all sides as if to crush him. The sheep moved closer; right up to him.

He reacted promptly. Springing to his feet, he pulled the horse in frantic haste to the bank, scrambled up and clambered into the saddle, kicked his patent-leather heels into its sides, and was off at a gallop, one hand on the reins and the other holding his hat so that it would not fly away, the empty stirrup irons dangling like helpless hands in all directions.

A keen gust of wind blew up, and all of a sudden a loud barking cry was heard, rebounding between the steep sides of the gorge; echoing all through the pass; until his head was full of the mournful cries of hungry foxes. It was still a fair distance to his workshop; still no farm to be seen, — he was on his own, somewhere deep in a pass among the fells.

Night visit

They came late at night, were noisy, and demanded fuel. There were two of them knocking at the door; one had blood on his face and had lost his jacket. The farmer was in bed, but he slipped on his clothes and hurried out. He was holding a torch, and he asked them to keep quiet; there were people asleep there.

"Country bastard," said the bloody one, "always sleeping. The country bastard never needs do anything but sleep. Just have his beauty sleep. Where's the woman?"

The farmer ignored his nonsense and turned to the other. He seemed sober and must be the driver.

"Where are you from?"

"South," said the driver throwing away his cigarette. The wind snatched it into the darkness and he watched the spark.

"Going far?" asked the farmer.

"I'm going straight back," said the driver. "They're staying."

The farmer had bent down to unlock the pump. He straightened and looked at the two men, forgetting the padlock.

"Staying?"

"Isn't this Gröf?" asked the driver turning up his fur collar. "They said they wanted to go to Gröf."

"Yes, it is Gröf," said the farmer slowly. He regarded the bloody one who shambled towards them by the pump, tripping on the paving stones of the yard.

"Bloody darkness," mumbled that individual. "Always darkness with the country bastard. Just have his beauty sleep. Oh Mamma!"

"Who is he, that one?" asked the farmer, knuckles tightening on torch.

"I don't know either of them," replied the driver. "All I know is that they're on a trawler and had plenty of booze with them. They paid for the journey in advance and told me to take them to Gröf."

"Where's the other?" asked the farmer.

"Asleep in the car," said the driver. "He's slept an hour and can't be woken."

The bloodstained individual approached them with a fixed grin on his face. Stepping up to the farmer he patted him vigorously on the shoulder.

"Corpse in the back," he burbled. "Corpse in the baggage-train. Corpse for the country bastard. We'll bury it on the hill. You'll lend us the hill to bury him, eh, and give us a hand with the digging?"

He pulled a bottle from the waistband of his trousers, took a swig and grimaced. Then he held out the bottle to the farmer.

"Drink!"

The farmer did not answer but gazed hopelessly at the drunken man. Then he turned to the driver.

"I don't care for this kind of delivery," he said.

The driver shrugged his shoulders.

"They paid," he said.

"I don't know them," said the farmer. "I don't know what they want here."

"Perhaps you'll recognise the dead one in the back," said the driver. "They were talking about some woman who lived here."

The farmer went over to the car and bent to look through the window, switched on his torch and peered into the car. Then he backed a couple of paces, as though afraid of hitting his head. Looking reluctantly at the driver he shook his head.

"I've never seen him before in my life," he said. "You must be mistaken."

The driver unscrewed the cap of the fuel tank with one hand in his pocket, glancing over his shoulder at the farmer and half closing his eyes against the wind.

"I have to get back at once," he said. "They told me they wanted to go to Gröf, and they've paid."

The bloodstained individual had started shivering violently and was struggling to get the bottle back into his trousers. He was buffetted by the wind, and tacked unsteadily over to the pump, where he took shelter.

"Is the country bastard going to let us stand out here?" he demanded, lips pursed. „Where's the woman? We've got to carry in the corpse. Hup, hup!"

"I want a fill straight away," said the driver.

"Aren't you going to look at your son-in-law, country bastard?" asked the bloody one, crouching with hands in pockets. "All the voyage back from Newfoundland he talked about nothing but the woman and the kid. We'll just bury him on the hill. Hup!"

" In don't know what you think you're doing here, in the middle of the night on a strange farm. I'll fill the car, but then you must clear out — all three of you!"

"Listen, old fellow," said the driver, "aren't you here to serve us with fuel?"

A light went on in the farmhouse and somebody came to the window. They looked in that direction, the farmer lifting both hands clasped about the torch to wipe his nose on the back of one. His trousers flapped about thin legs and his feet were bare in his slippers.

"Are you going to let me stand here all night?" asked the driver.

The farmer did not answer but gazed at the house. Somebody was now standing in the open doorway, silhouetted in the dim light from within. It was a woman with a coat thrown over her shoulders.

"What is it, Pabbi?" she called.

„Nothing, girl. Just men wanting their car filled," the farmer called back. Then he turned to the driver. "You've managed to wake everybody. We've better things to do than to be tending drunks from the south."

The driver turned his fur collar up to his ears again.

"Do I get the car filled, or don't I?"

The farmer bent down and began to fumble with the padlock.

"After that you clear off with both of them," he commanded.

The driver made no reply. Standing with the cap of the fuel tank in one hand he watched his passenger tacking towards the door and almost falling on the way. The farmer straightened, staring silently after the man as he stumbled on, then looked at the driver and said, "It was enough for me when she came slinking home with that brat of hers."

The driver said nothing, but released the nozzle and inserted it in the tank.

"Shall I pump?" he asked.

The farmer started pumping without a reply; rapidly at first, but then with long, heavy strokes, swaying his whole body back and forth, but not moving his eyes from the door of the house. The man had reached the door and was talking with the woman, though their words could not be heard.

"Infernally windy tonight," remarked the driver becoming affable. „There was a bloody sandstorm out on the flats, right in our faces. I once had a windscreen ruined there."

"You want it full?" asked the farmer shortly.

"Yes, I'll pump now," answered the driver and approached the pump. "The lads are on a trawler, so they'll hardly stop long with you. But they paid for the trip and asked to come here. Now I'll pump."

But the farmer showed no signs of intending to release the

handle He exerted himself to pump with increased vigour, spitting into the darkness and constantly watching the door. The drunk was shuffling on the doorstep, still talking to the woman and making gestures with his arms. The wind carried snatches of his words to them: ". . . corpse in the baggage-train . . . borrow the hill . . . Newfoundland bank . . . the kid . . . country bastard."

"Damned savages!" said the farmer.

"They soak it up when they come ashore," said the driver. "May have been a whole month at sea. It's a dog's life."

"It was enough for me when she brought that brat of hers home," said the farmer, breathless from pumping.

The drunk had now sat down on the doorstep and pulled out his bottle, while the woman walked over to the pump. She was wearing a large coat over her nightdress. She was agitated and clasped her arms tightly about herself, turning her back into the wind.

"Pabbi," she cried, "he says it's Steini."

"I don't know any blasted Steini." said the farmer pumping harder.

"Let me pump now," said the driver stretching out his hand. "You've done enough."

"Steini," said the daughter. "You know, Tiny Tot's daddy. He's come all this way."

"And in a fine state, too," snapped the farmer.

The woman turned to her car and looked through the window. Taking hold of the doorhandle she said, "He always drank so badly, once he'd tasted a drop."

"Go inside, girl, and don't be catching your death," said the farmer, whose pumping was now beginning to slow down. "I'm filling the car for the men and then they're going — all three of them."

"Yes, Pabbi, but I didn't think Steini ever wanted to see me again," said the girl, who had already opened the car door.

"It doesn't look as if he's going to see the hell of a lot

of you now, in the state he is," snarled the farmer, and he stopped pumping, though he still held on to the handle and leaned against the pump.

"He'll be all right in the morning when he's slept it off," she said looking at her father.

"Maybe he will, but he'll be back in the south by then," he said.

"I'll pump the rest," said the driver, taking hold of the handle. "Let me have a bill and I'll be off like a shot."

The farmer surrendered the pump-handle without moving out of the way, and the driver had difficulty in standing so that he could use his muscles to the full. He made no attempt to push the farmer away.

"Yes, I'll let you have a bill. Girl, run in and make out a bill, since you're out of bed anyway! And be sharp about it; these men are in a hurry to get back!"

She leaned forward into the car, then looked back at her father.

"But Pabbi, you can't mean . . . now that Steini's come at last. And I thought he didn't want to have anything more to do with me."

"It was enough for me when you came back from the south with that brat, you foolish girl."

"I don't understand you, Pabbi. And you're so fond of Tiny Tot. He won't be with anyone but you. And Steini's his daddy."

She stooped over the unconscious passanger in the back of the car. "Oh my God, there's blood on his face. Has anything happened?"

The driver had stopped pumping and was screwing the cap on the fuel thank.

"They got out to piss on the way," he said, "and they started fighting. They both fell down and grazed themselves, but I separated them. It's nothing."

He hurried over to the girl, took hold of the sleeping passenger's shoulder and shook him vigorously.

"Wake up! Wake up, man! You're there!"

The girl put an arm round the man's neck and lifted one of his eyelids, but it was no use. He murmured something and his tongue appeared at the corner of his mouth. Vomit had run down his chin and there was an unpleasant odour from him. The driver took hold of his shoulders and dragged him forward so that one leg hung through the door.

"I've told you already, they're going back," said the farmer with some heat. "People can't just drive up to strange farms in the middle of the night and leave any sort of scum behind them. I'm master here, do you hear that?"

He held the driver by the shoulder and clenched his fist.

"They paid for the trip and asked to come here," said the driver calmly. "It's none of my business."

"I have my rights and I'm not having anything to do with these wretches," cried the farmer, his voice beginning to shake.

"Pabbi, you can't shut Steini out," cried the girl. "He's Tiny Tot's daddy, that you're so fond of, and I never expected to see him again."

The driver had dragged the passenger out of the car and humped him down by the fuel pump before the farmer could do anything about it. Then he pulled some money out of his pocket and handed it to him. The farmer showed no inclination to accept it, but stared in turn at the driver and the man who lay in a heap by the pump. The girl was fumbling over him.

"You take him back with you," he cried, pounding his fists together. "I'll have you know I'm master here."

The driver pushed the bundle of notes hurriedly into the girl's hand, pulled on his gloves and jumped into the car. The engine burst into life at once, and he stepped on the pedal so that its roar drowned the noise of the wind. The farmer ran forward and caught hold of the car by the radio aerial.

"Pabbi, don't! You'll be run down," cried the girl, and she ran to her father and caught hold of his arm. This enabled the driver to start off down the track. He drove slowly and tried to watch father and daughter for fear of hitting them.

The drunk had now stood up by the doorstep and started staggering towards them.

"Now we'll bury him on the hill . . . get a spade and dig . . . country bastard can have his beauty sleep . . . ought to be on a trawler . . . Hup, hup!"

For a while the old farmer stood as if at a loss, staring first at his daughter and then at the drunken seaman. After that he walked to the unconscious figure by the pump and bent over it. He grasped the man under the arms from behind and began to drag him in the direction of the farm. The daughter ran after him and took hold of the man's legs, but could not lift them. For a moment the farmer stopped, straightened his back and stretched himself, blowing and breathless. Then he bent again, grasped Steini as before, and struggled towards the door with him, ignoring the stones in the yard. He dragged him in short bursts at a time, his chest heaving with the exertion. His daughter followed, holding the feet of her child's father, while his shipmate brought up the rear, crying, "Hup, hup!"

Near the door the farmer straightened himself again to get his breath, rubbing the small of his back, and he looked at his daughter and said:

"Didn't you think it was enough, with that brat from the south?"

Then he bent down over the man again.

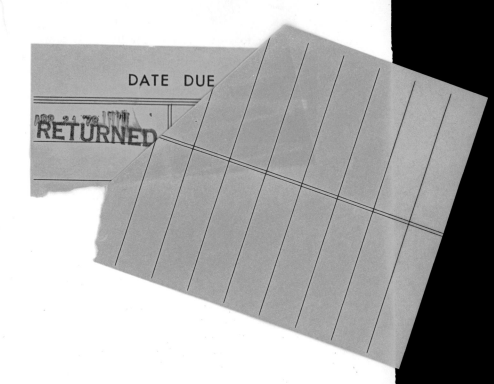